Contents

Stories from Pulp Fiction's Golden Age

A ND it *was* a golden age.

The 1930s and 1940s were a vibrant, seminal time for a gigantic audience of eager readers, probably the largest per capita audience of readers in American history. The magazine racks were chock-full of publications with ragged trims, garish cover art, cheap brown pulp paper, low cover prices—and the most excitement you could hold in your hands.

"Pulp" magazines, named for their rough-cut, pulpwood paper, were a vehicle for more amazing tales than Scheherazade could have told in a million and one nights. Set apart from higher-class "slick" magazines, printed on fancy glossy paper with quality artwork and superior production values, the pulps were for the "rest of us," adventure story after adventure story for people who liked to *read*. Pulp fiction authors were no-holds-barred entertainers—real storytellers. They were more interested in a thrilling plot twist, a horrific villain or a white-knuckle adventure than they were in lavish prose or convoluted metaphors.

The sheer volume of tales released during this wondrous golden age remains unmatched in any other period of literary history—hundreds of thousands of published stories in over nine hundred different magazines. Some titles lasted only an issue or two; many magazines succumbed to paper shortages during World War II, while others endured for decades yet. Pulp fiction remains as a treasure trove of stories you can read, stories you can love, stories you can remember. The stories were driven by plot and character, with grand heroes, terrible villains, beautiful damsels (often in distress), diabolical plots, amazing places, breathless romances. The readers wanted to be taken beyond the mundane, to live adventures far removed from their ordinary lives—and the pulps rarely failed to deliver.

In that regard, pulp fiction stands in the tradition of all memorable literature. For as history has shown, good stories are much more than fancy prose. William Shakespeare, Charles Dickens, Jules Verne, Alexandre Dumas—many of the greatest literary figures wrote their fiction for the readers, not simply literary colleagues and academic admirers. And writers for pulp magazines were no exception. These publications reached an audience that dwarfed the circulations of today's short story magazines. Issues of the pulps were scooped up and read by over thirty million avid readers each month.

Because pulp fiction writers were often paid no more than a cent a word, they had to become prolific or starve. They also had to write aggressively. As Richard Kyle, publisher and editor of *Argosy,* the first and most long-lived of the pulps, so pointedly explained: "The pulp magazine writers, the best of them, worked for markets that did not write for critics or attempt to satisfy timid advertisers. Not having to answer to anyone other than their readers, they wrote about human beings on the edges of the unknown, in those new lands the future would explore. They wrote for what we would become, not for what we had already been."

Some of the more lasting names that graced the pulps include H. P. Lovecraft, Edgar Rice Burroughs, Robert E. Howard, Max Brand, Louis L'Amour, Elmore Leonard, Dashiell Hammett, Raymond Chandler, Erle Stanley Gardner, John D. MacDonald, Ray Bradbury, Isaac Asimov, Robert Heinlein—and, of course, L. Ron Hubbard.

In a word, he was among the most prolific and popular writers of the era. He was also the most enduring—hence this series—and certainly among the most legendary. It all began only months after he first tried his hand at fiction, with L. Ron Hubbard tales appearing in *Thrilling Adventures, Argosy, Five-Novels Monthly, Detective Fiction Weekly, Top-Notch, Texas Ranger, War Birds, Western Stories,* even *Romantic Range.* He could write on any subject, in any genre, from jungle explorers to deep-sea divers, from G-men and gangsters, cowboys and flying aces to mountain climbers, hard-boiled detectives and spies. But he really began to shine when he turned his talent to science fiction and fantasy of which he authored nearly fifty novels or novelettes to forever change the shape of those genres.

Following in the tradition of such famed authors as Herman Melville, Mark Twain, Jack London and Ernest Hemingway, Ron Hubbard actually lived adventures that his own characters would have admired—as an ethnologist among primitive tribes, as prospector and engineer in hostile climes, as a captain of vessels on four oceans. He even wrote a series of articles for *Argosy,* called "Hell Job," in which he lived and told of the most dangerous professions a man could put his hand to.

Finally, and just for good measure, he was also an accomplished photographer, artist, filmmaker, musician and educator. But he was first and foremost a *writer,* and that's the L. Ron Hubbard we come to know through the pages of this volume.

This library of Stories from the Golden Age presents the best of L. Ron Hubbard's fiction from the heyday of storytelling, the Golden Age of the pulp magazines. In these eighty volumes, readers are treated to a full banquet of 153 stories, a kaleidoscope of tales representing every imaginable genre: science fiction, fantasy, western, mystery, thriller, horror, even romance—action of all kinds and in all places.

Because the pulps themselves were printed on such inexpensive paper with high acid content, issues were not meant to endure. As the years go by, the original issues of every pulp from *Argosy* through *Zeppelin Stories* continue crumbling into brittle, brown dust. This library preserves the L. Ron Hubbard tales from that era, presented with a distinctive look that brings back the nostalgic flavor of those times.

L. Ron Hubbard's Stories from the Golden Age has something for every taste, every reader. These tales will return you to a time when fiction was good clean entertainment and the most fun a kid could have on a rainy afternoon or the best thing an adult could enjoy after a long day at work.

Pick up a volume, and remember what reading is supposed to be all about. Remember curling up with a *great story.*

—Kevin J. Anderson

KEVIN J. ANDERSON *is the author of more than ninety critically acclaimed works of speculative fiction, including The Saga of Seven Suns, the continuation of the Dune Chronicles with Brian Herbert, and his* New York Times *bestselling novelization of L. Ron Hubbard's* Ai! Pedrito!

The Dive Bomber

CHAPTER ONE

Once the Tops

L OOK here, Mr. O'Neal, I can't let you kill yourself with that ship!"

Lucky Martin said it earnestly and loyally and, as he always did, he meant just exactly what he said. And, as Number One test pilot in the United States, Lucky Martin's opinions on the subject of ships was not commonly thrust aside.

But the instant he uttered those words he knew that he could have said nothing worse. No profanity could have goaded O'Neal into the rage which swelled him out to the red bursting point.

"So, you too!" roared Big Tom O'Neal. "And I thought you were my friend. I know now. You've been talking about it, you're the one that started it. . . . Who the hell built this ship, anyway?"

"You did," said Lucky Martin, in despair.

"Who tested the first bomber the Navy ever bought?"

"You did," gulped Lucky Martin.

"Of course I did, but you and all the others are yammering about how old I'm getting. I'm forty-six, see? Forty-six isn't old! I've got my transport, haven't I? I passed the last Department physical, didn't I? And I'm the oldest test pilot in the business, ain't I? And who owns O'Neal Aircraft Company? I ask you that!"

"You do," said Lucky very miserably.

"There, you admit I'm competent to test my own ship before these people."

"Sure . . . but—"

"But what, you whelp?"

Lucky sent an appealing glance to Dixie O'Neal and she needed no urging to intercede. Dixie, knowing that one of these two men would have to test the ship and loving them equally, she threw her strength on the side of the one who might be expected to come out best—Lucky Martin.

"Dad, you're too old for grandstanding. You ought to know better. Nobody questions your ability. Lucky is here to do this work and you know what they said about your heart. Don't try the gravity test, please, Dad. You know that's how men get killed. They go out like . . ."

Big, blustering, ungainly Tom O'Neal, renowned for a stubborn disposition, took this as a new affront. Seeing that Lucky and Dixie had united forces, instead of bowing gracefully, he let his anger get away from him entirely.

He blasted them with a voice three times louder than a Cyclone in a dive. He told them they were impertinent, that they were hardly dry behind the ears, that their opinions carried less weight than a Duralumin girder and that their skulls were filled with the purest of ozone.

He was very unjust. Lucky Martin had not come by his own reputation without ample merit and, as everybody knew the length and breadth of the Atlantic seaboard, Dixie O'Neal was as bright as she was beautiful, which savored of hyperbole.

Stung by the fact that he *was* getting old and that he was no longer considered the best in the business, Tom O'Neal forgot that his prominence was at present wholly based on his ownership of this big plant, and upon his cunning in designing of fighting ships for the Army and Navy.

Through the office door they could all see the restless crowd which stood on the edge of the field—a crowd which waited in the full expectancy of seeing a man die that day.

Tom O'Neal settled the argument by picking up his helmet and goggles and, glaring at his daughter and his future son-in-law, stalked out toward the waiting dive bomber.

Commander Lawson stopped him for an instant and shook his hand. "Hope it goes all right, Tom. Lucky off his feed?"

"Damn Lucky," growled O'Neal. "He says I'm getting too old."

"But out of respect for Dixie—" began Lawson.

"Damn Dixie!"

Scandalized, the kind-faced, portly naval officer blinked his sea-faded eyes at the aircraft ahead, and went two-thirds speed astern and out of the slipstream which was beginning to blast back from the prop.

Lucky Martin, looking down in spirit and rather hopeless, loafed out of the office, hands in his pockets, helmet buckle dangling beside his square jaw.

He was six feet tall, but his shoulders were so broad that he looked to be of average height until he walked through and towered over a crowd. The only thing which marred his looks was a scar running from his chin to his ear, put there by a shed wing which had almost torn his head off before he could get out of the plummeting fuselage. The scar marred his beauty, but infinitely increased the glamour which hung about him.

His was a profession in which men are often killed thoroughly. But unlike those test pilots who merchandise their danger, Lucky had very little to say and a great deal to do. He did his job efficiently and well and if it had not been for the scar he would have passed anywhere for an especially good-looking boxer or sailor or ditch digger or a cop or movie actor.

O'Neal kicked the gun with the heel of his hand and sent the dive bomber skidding around into takeoff position. With a triumphant glare at Lucky, O'Neal pushed the stick into the panel, took his heels off the brakes and went away from there like a shot silver arrow—which might or might not fall in one piece.

"He's a brave man," said Lucky in appreciation, trying to appear calm and light a cigarette, but unable to make the match and smoke connect.

"He's a damned fool!" said Commander Lawson.

"Is there any difference?" replied Lucky.

"None," said Dixie, coming up and trying hard to keep the tension out of her husky voice, obeying the flying code by being excited at nothing.

The group of officers, mechanics, civilians, pilots and a couple of state troopers who had come down from the highway above watched the stubby little ship snarl skyward for altitude.

Once in a while somebody sighed explosively and immediately

looked embarrassed. People tried to talk about things which didn't matter, only to find that they didn't matter after all. Restless and expecting the worst, but hoping for the best, the crowd stared until necks ached and the dive bomber became only an occasional sparkle of wings in the dazzling blue of the cloudless sky.

Dixie frayed the corner of a small red handkerchief and, without taking her eyes from the faraway, droning flash, reached out and took hold of Lucky's arm as though to steady herself.

"He's all right," said Lucky, finding his throat dry.

"Sure he is," said Dixie, never once losing sight of the ship now ten thousand feet above them.

"It's a good plane," said Commander Lawson. "Took all its other tests in top shape. But I don't think it can stand . . . I mean, sure it will. The Navy needs a dive bomber like that. Never did have a good one. Wings always folding back on them. Takes real stamina for a ship to stick in the groove and come out without losing anything but its bombs. A ten-thousand-foot dive at terminal velocity is too much for any . . . I mean, sure it will."

"You bet," said a strange fellow Lucky had not so far noticed.

"You know Mr. Bullard, Martin?" said Lawson.

Lucky looked sideways to find a man who was as tall as he was but who weighed at least two hundred pounds more. Bullard's fat looked like it had been hung on him roll by roll. His brows bulged over small, quick eyes. His jaw protruded loosely, hiding his collar and tie. His paunch looked as though he had moored a blimp to his belt and let some of the helium

7

out. A giant who rumbled rather than talked, who grinned eternally, Bullard possessed a heartiness which was too studied to be casual.

"Hello," said Lucky, looking back up at the ship.

"The great Lucky Martin," said Bullard, taking the pilot's hard palm in the fat folds of his own and shaking it. "Well, this is a pleasure. I hear you're to be the next boss in case anything happens. . . ."

Lucky looked steadily into the shifty eyes. "What did you say?"

"I said you're sure Lucky, you sure deserve that name. Is this the pretty lady you're going to marry? Well, well, Lucky is putting it much too mild. Always good politics to marry the daughter of . . ."

The crack of Lucky's backhand against the fat mouth jarred the otherwise silent field.

Bullard's eyes glowed redly, but he grinned and bowed and scraped. "I didn't mean any harm, Mr. Martin. I'm sorry I said it, though it did . . ."

"He's coming down!" yelled a mechanic named Lefty Flynn.

Forgotten was Bullard. The song of the dive bomber's engine had been a soft whisper before. Now the sound began to rise in pitch and volume, to a hoarse roar, upward to a rasping snarl, and higher still to a shrill, hammering scream which stabbed down and bludgeoned the field.

The dive bomber had gone over the hump. Nose pointing straight at the earth, eighteen thousand feet down, engine on full, building up to terminal velocity when the resistance of the wind equaled the downward drive of the wide-open throttle.

From a dot against the blue, the ship swiftly became a silver cross inverted. Larger and larger, doubling in size with each passing second, the plane was hurling itself toward the checkerboard of earth, to seemingly certain destruction.

But this was not dangerous. The buildings shook with the flood of sound, ears deafened and closed. But this was not the worst. In a moment O'Neal would pull out and then the danger would come.

To jerk a ship level from a downward speed of seven miles a minute or more would put a strain of nine times the plane's weight on the wings. From two hundred pounds, the pilot's weight would be instantaneously stepped to eighteen hundred pounds, every ounce of which would be bent on crushing him into his pit. Men's brains came loose in their skulls when the pullout was too sharp. Wings came off when the gravity increased to eleven. Over that men became a senseless, bleeding mass, smashed into their cockpit.

"He knows what he's doing," prayed Lucky into the din.

"The ship can take it," whispered Dixie.

Three thousand feet up, still howling straight at the earth, the dive bomber was due to level out.

Lucky would have given ten years of his life to have been in that plane instead of O'Neal. Up there it was too loud and hectic to think. Down here it was terrible.

The plane's nose pulled up slightly, fighting the inertia which strove to dash the silver wings to fragments against the dusty earth.

Abruptly the ship snapped level.

For an instant it sped straight out toward the horizon and

then, as though a bomb had exploded between the struts, it flew into countless bits of wreckage which sailed in a scattering cloud about the fuselage.

"Her wings!" yelled Lawson. "Bail out! Good God, he's trapped!"

They could see O'Neal's head. He raised one hand. He strove to pry himself out of the plunging coffin which, with renewed speed was darting straight down again.

He might have made it if he had had another thousand feet.

Belt unbuckled, blasted back against the seat, O'Neal stayed where he was, half out of his pit, until the gleaming fuselage vanished into the earth, leaving a spreading cloud of twisted metal fragments to mingle with the hovering dust.

The silence which ensued was cut only by the soft patter of wreckage settling on the field.

People broke free from the paralysis of horror and began to run toward the plane. The crash siren screamed and an ambulance leaped toward the spot where no ambulance was needed.

Dixie tried to follow but could not. A mechanic's wife gently put her arm across the girl's shoulders and turned her face away from the lazy, curling dust.

Lucky was standing on the edge of the pit, looking down through the smoke. The banks had caved, quenching any fire, burying O'Neal.

Lucky wiped his hands across his face and slid over the shifting clay, searching for the cockpit.

CHAPTER TWO

But to Sell to Another Country

A week after the funeral, Commander Lawson called at the silent O'Neal Aircraft plant.

He found Lucky Martin thumbing through cluttered files in the main office. Dixie O'Neal was sitting on the window seat, looking out across the field. Her dark eyes were sad and her face, in startling contrast to her jet hair, was as pale as ivory. Her small hands twisted nervously at a scrap of paper.

Lawson shook Lucky's hand and greeted Dixie and, although he was friendly enough, Lucky could sense a certain reserve, the inflexibility of an officer who has a duty to perform.

"We'll go ahead on another diver as soon as I get financial affairs straight," said Lucky, running harried fingers through his curly and unruly brown hair. "I'm a lot handier with a stick than I am with an adding machine."

"Aren't your clerks . . . ?"

"There are no clerks," said Lucky, waving his hand at the empty outer room.

"But certainly O'Neal's engineers—"

"I'm the engineers," said Lucky.

"Why, what's the matter?"

"We're strapped for cash, and I couldn't sales-talk the bankers. I guess I'm better behind a panel than behind a desk."

"That's unfortunate," said Lawson, squirming slightly, but still trying not to look gray and severe.

"But I think we can swing it," said Lucky with a hopeful grin. "You know doggone well your Navy couldn't get along without our dive bomber. The whole new fighting technique is built around this ship. While I don't expect you to advance anything, your support and okay would certainly help me smooth things over with the bankers. O'Neal left a couple of thousand, but that's all."

"But good heavens, Martin, you can't mean your other contracts failed to bring you in money. There's that Army pursuit job you built and—"

"Money all gone to satisfy old accounts. Money expended on the development of a new metal. The steel companies wouldn't help, you know. They need volume before they can develop anything. We've got enough spare parts we used for testing and enough experience on this job to make another one like it. Dixie—"

"After all, Miss O'Neal, you're the boss around here now," said Lawson. "What do you think of this idea to build another one?"

Dixie faced the commander for an instant and then, gradually, the vitality faded out of her again. "What's the use? Dad would have wanted Lucky to carry on. This dive bomber was a ten-year dream and three years of labor . . . but . . . Lucky could get a job with Eastern Air if he wanted. He could . . . I'm sorry. Of course we'll go on."

Lawson shifted uncomfortably again. He cleared his throat two or three times. "As a matter of fact . . . er . . . Martin, there's no need of your wasting further time on the dive bomber."

Lucky came out of his swivel chair and braced himself with flat hands against the blotter and papers. "What are you trying to tell me?"

"Damn it all," said Lawson, wishing he was back on a bridge and in uniform, "I hate to have to tell you this. We saw the dive bomber. You claim it to have pursuit ship qualities. You claim it has a long-range cruising radius. You claim speed. You claim it will hold together in a twelve-thousand-foot power dive better than any ship ever before built."

"Certainly we claim it, and we'll prove it. Something went wrong, Commander. Something's haywire about that ship, but we'll straighten it out."

"Martin, that thing is a killer, and will always be a killer. It's an engine with ears tacked to it, horsepower without wings. The Navy will have nothing further to do with it. Your next ship might hold, but what about the production ships? Our men are valuable. We can't risk—"

"See here," begged Lucky. "One try doesn't mean failure. Other ships—"

"There are other ships on the market which *will* hold together in a power dive. Take Miss O'Neal's advice and quit before you're killed, Martin."

Lucky sat down suddenly. But he was by no means beaten. Calmly he said, "Commander, I'm going to build this ship if I have to rob a bank, and I'm going to sell it to the Navy and you're going to buy a round hundred of them on the first order."

"I tell you—"

"Lucky," said Dixie quietly, "why can't you ever see when you're beaten? It's folly to go ahead and—" She stopped, studying his face. She turned slowly to Lawson. "It's no use talking to him, Commander. And Dad would have wanted it this way."

Lawson had delivered himself of his orders and he was glad to withdraw. Lucky stared long at the door which had let the officer through.

"I guess I'm kind of yellow, Lucky. But I don't think I can stand any more of it. The first one you tested broke up before you had it all the way through its common flight tests. The next one killed . . . Dad. Aren't you being stubborn? Can't you see that everything is set against you? No clerks, no engineers, only one mechanic left, no money. Someday I hoped you'd beat the game by quitting before it got you. I hoped you'd get an airline job and we could get a place in Washington—a little place and a flivver."

"You'll have your little place," said Lucky, smiling. "Sure you will . . . Dixie. And once I get the Navy convinced . . ."

Lefty Flynn, the last remaining mechanic, who now functioned as both janitor and office boy, stuck his thick head through the door.

"There's a couple gents hanging around outside," said Lefty. "One looks like he needs a mooring mast, and the other is stinky with perfume. Do I let 'em in or knock 'em out?" He showed, as he rubbed his smudged pug nose, that he infinitely preferred the latter course.

"Let them in," said Lucky.

"Aw . . . all right. Hey, you birds, this way!"

Mr. Bullard squeezed through the door and stood beaming before the desk. A man almost as thick as Mr. Bullard's right arm stood hidden behind the column of Mr. Bullard's leg.

"Well, well, well!" said Mr. Bullard, heartily overlooking the tension of Lucky's evident dislike. "Mr. Martin, meet Mr. Smith."

The man whose name was not Smith offered Lucky a limp hand.

Bullard was evidently to be spokesman. He declined a chair which had not been offered and, clearing his throat like an elephant blows out its trunk, said, "Well, well, well, a touching picture. Well, can I understand the hopelessness with which you are faced, Lucky."

"Mr. Martin," corrected Lucky.

"Yes, of course, Mr. Martin. But it is darkest before the dawn, calmest before the tempest, sunniest after the storm—"

"And all is not gold that glitters," said Lucky. "What do you want?"

"Why, to help you, of course. I . . . I mean, Mr. Martin, in me you see the Good Samaritan, the solver of all problems, the balm to all ills. In short, Mr. Martin, in me you will have salvation."

"Thanks."

"Oh, don't thank me yet. Mr. Martin, how would you like to have me finance the building of one hundred dive bombers?"

"Where's the catch?"

"No catch. I turn over the money up to and including five million dollars, and you build the ships. That's all."

15

"Can you do card tricks, too?" said Lucky.

"No, but I sing a winning song, Mr. Martin. Five million dollars would buy a place in Paradise, so it would. And all you have to do is—"

"Turn it down."

Bullard blinked on that one. He had caught it in the teeth and it winded him a trifle. But he swelled again to his usual size, and smiled good-naturedly. "Of course you'll have your joke."

"Listen," said Lucky. "I don't know you, and I don't want to know you, but before we turn this down, let me put it up to the person with the real authority here. How about it, Dixie? Do we bite or what?"

Dixie's study of Bullard and the man called Smith had already formed her answer. She shook her head.

"What would you do with a hundred dive bombers?" said Lucky.

"Why . . . use them, of course. My boy . . . I mean, Mr. Martin, when a man's country lets him down. . . ."

"I get it," said Lucky. "You're hoping I'll forget the new Neutrality Laws. Bullard, the government of the United States of America recently enacted a measure which says, in effect, that no pursuit or other plane of any kind shall be exported from the United States until it is two years old. Otherwise, in the event of a war, the United States would have to compete, most likely, against its own ingenuity. I happen to be an American, Bullard, or hadn't you heard?"

"But they've let you down!" cried Bullard, shaking fleshily with amazement. "Three years' work—"

The shadow named Smith reared up level with the top of the desk and piped shrilly, "Give him the other barrel, Joe."

"Okay. Okay, I'll give him the other barrel. Look here, Martin. If you will come to a certain country and build in their aircraft plants three hundred of these dive bombers, you will be handed one million dollars to the penny, every kopek of it US cash dough, in return for your services."

"That is a good bargain," said Lucky. "But it has just occurred to me why these dive bombers are such good planes, Bullard. You know, a couple squadrons of them, flying at twenty thousand feet, out of sight of the sea, could sight the enemy ships before those ships can get the range."

"Of course," said Bullard, eagerly. "You bet."

"And then," continued Lucky, "these two squadrons or so go over the hump and start their dive straight down, at a speed of seven miles a minute, too fast to be hit."

"Sure. That's right."

"About two thousand feet above the water, or even less, the bombers prepare to level out. They trip their toggles and down go their bombs, to blow the battleships to smithereens. At that altitude there can be few misses, and the bomber is gone before many shots can be fired. You get it, Bullard?"

"Sure I do."

"No you don't," said Lucky. "O'Neal dive bombers will never be used to sink the battleships of the United States Navy. Now you can get out."

Bullard shed the mask, if such it was. Bitter and crafty, he leaned forward. "Okay, Lucky Martin. Okay. But don't forget that someday you are going to manufacture those planes, and don't forget that, when the time comes, you'll crawl to us on your knees. You can't get away from us, Lucky Martin."

"I said to get out."

Bullard made no move. "The other day you slapped me. Now today—"

"Joe!" yelled Smith, in alarm.

The cry served warning to Lucky. He ducked back and Bullard's palm met only empty air.

Lucky went over the desk like a high jumper. He snatched Bullard and booted him through the door.

Blue steel flashed in Smith's hand. A monkey wrench sailed through the door and knocked down the gun. Flynn, following up his wrench, swooped down upon Smith and sent him soaring in the wake of Bullard.

The unsavory pair scrambled into their car. Safe behind the wheel, clutch ready to let out, Bullard shouted, "You'll be sorry for this, you fool! You don't know what I can do. I've got influence and, plenty of it! You think you've seen the last of me, do you?" With an angry snort, Bullard rocketed the car out of sight.

"We licked 'em, boss," said the happy Flynn.

"Yeah," said Lucky with a weary sigh. "For how long?"

Dixie turned puzzled eyes upon Lucky. "The man must be insane to make such an offer. Even if we did make the ships for him he could never get them out of the United States without the government knowing about it."

"The only way he could do that," said Lucky, sinking into a chair, "would be to have the rating changed on the type."

"But he couldn't do that!"

18

"Okay. But don't forget that someday you are going to
manufacture those planes, and don't forget that,
when the time comes, you'll crawl to us on your knees."

"If I fail to show the government what a fine ship this is, he could. And unless I *do* build this bomber and make a success of it, or if I build it and crash it in the tests—"

"He might be able to export it?" said Dixie. "Export a fighting plane?"

"Not as a fighting plane," said Lucky with a worried scowl.

"You mean there's a chance that it could be exported in spite of the laws?" said Dixie.

"Yes. The law only applies to fighting planes. The government's rejection of a ship as unfit for war work removes it from the class of military airplanes. The only way a military airplane can be exported is after it has been used for two years."

"You wouldn't think the government would run a chance like that," said Dixie.

"You mean having someday to fight equipment built in the United States? They can't accept everything," said Lucky. "And they pull a lot of boners from time to time. I guess they can't help it. You know what happened in the case of the Thompson submachine gun. Thompson, an American, offered it to the United States government, but it was turned down. Thompson was then forced to sell his blueprints and rights to the British government, who accepted it and made it a standard weapon for British forces. Someday there's a chance American troops will be killed with that very weapon."

"But if the Navy turns us down, what's wrong with selling elsewhere?" persisted Dixie.

"I'm funny. First, I'm a Yank and then I'm a test pilot. There's a nice point of ethics here, but I wouldn't be able to look at the flag again if I placed a potent fighting machine in the hands of another nation, where it will someday be used against the warships of the United States."

"Never mind," said Dixie, "it won't ever come to that. We'll sell it to the United States. We'll make it better than the last one we built. The Navy will take it. We won't let Bullard in on this." Some of the old zest was with her again.

CHAPTER THREE

A Great Plane, Ready for the Test

WITH no visible assets but his own ability, Lucky Martin stubbornly set out to finance the construction of another dive bomber.

Dixie, a more earthbound being and therefore infinitely more sane than the pilot, helped him all she could, once she understood that nothing could stop him.

Lucky Martin snapped at a job in Cincinnati, worked six days, took a scheduled pursuit job through its paces without taking it apart and returned East with fifteen hundred dollars cash and an aching pair of ears. The earache disappeared, so did the fifteen hundred, but a down payment had been made on an engine.

Dixie met a steel executive and, in return for a few minutes' conversation, received a half ton of alloy.

Lucky wrote glowing letters and received, in return, a special prop, a new type of retractable landing gear and half a dozen instruments.

Flynn got into a crap game and won fifty dollars which was immediately turned into the treasury.

Dixie sold her custom-built roadster for half its value and parted with a mink coat and mortgaged the only thing O'Neal had left clear to her—his sixteen-room, four-bath, three-garage mansion.

Lucky turned up at Miami, borrowed a ship from a millionaire friend and took first prize in an air show, enriching the stake by five thousand.

Although she had very little faith in the project itself, Dixie had much faith in her pilot. Perhaps she could not find it in her heart to see him fail and, again, perhaps she knew that the quicker disaster came, the sooner Lucky Martin would become Pilot Martin on EAT.

Three months after O'Neal's death found the plant going once more. Clerks added columns of figures, engineers slid their slip sticks, mechanics hammered and swore.

On the platform in the shop, the new dive bomber began to take shape.

Unique in construction, it could carry almost half its own weight in deadly missiles. It had two cockpits, both covered with a glass hood, accommodating pilot, gunner, and a new .50-caliber machine gun aft, and two thirty-thirty machine guns on either wing.

A flying fortress, it was no larger than the pursuit planes of yesterday and a fleet of them could be expected to wipe out the largest flotilla on the seas.

Midway in the hurried construction, with Lucky almost out on his feet from weariness, threatened disaster came from a new quarter.

The blueprints of the plane were assembled in books, making a considerable pile. These were almost always in use and therefore it was impossible to keep their precious pages under lock and key.

One night Lucky was working late. The only man with

him was Flynn. Around them and the single globe of yellow light, the shop stretched out in gloomy darkness.

Lucky, puzzling over the retracting gear, sent Flynn to the office for the book covering it.

Ever since Bullard had tried so hard to force them into a deal, Flynn had never neglected to carry a spanner. He had it now, jutting out of his hip pocket, about three times the size of an automatic.

He was whistling because it was dark and because the shop was so lonely and still and the whistle was a tuneless thing which made the dimness more lonesome than ever.

Flynn pushed back the door of the unlighted office. Something rustled just in front of him. Flynn dived to the left, trying to get his silhouette out of the light behind him.

An automatic roared, strewing the bullet's path with sparks.

Flynn on the floor. The spanner came out and over his head like a grenade. It clinked hard as it hit.

A loud curse of mingled profanity and pain accompanied the clatter of the falling gun. Flynn's aim had been true.

Lucky sprinted across the littered floor, hurdling parts and crates.

"Look out!" shouted Flynn. "He had a gun!"

Lucky turned at right angles and raced out of the shop. He turned along the outside of the building and came up to the window of the office.

A man, a shadow in the starlight, was half in and half out of the opening.

Lucky seized his collar. The shadow unloaded itself off the sill and, smashing out with terrified fists, knocked Lucky loose.

25

For a moment they grappled. Lucky tripped and sprawled on the ground. His still-reaching fingers touched leather and he hauled a valise down with him.

Flynn had found the automatic. Leaning out of the window, he fired twice into the air.

The trespasser vanished.

When Lucky had found the lights, and when hangars and field glowed cheerily, he examined his prize and discovered a complete set of blueprint books inside.

"It's that Bullard," said Flynn, rubbing a bruised elbow.

"Whoever it is, that was close. After this, these things are going to stay in the safe at night."

"You bet!"

"And," said Lucky, "you'd better carry a gun around."

Flynn caressed his spanner. "No sir, this little baby did all the work that was needed."

Lucky grinned as he put the books away. "I guess that ought to discourage that free balloon. In three weeks we'll be finished, and if he can do anything in that time, let him try."

"Yeah," said Flynn. "Let him."

In the turmoil of last-minute checks, Bullard was completely forgotten. The dive bomber spread its wings and gleamed before its proud creators and only one other incident, so trivial that it was completely forgotten until later, occurred to mar the efficiency of the building.

Lucky, on the next to the last day, was up at dawn to find four mechanics, including Flynn, already on the job. As Lucky walked about the ship, giving it a semi-final check, he stepped on a wing bolt, which rolled under his boot, almost throwing him. He leaned over to toss it away.

"Say, Flynn," said Lucky, "I thought we had an exact number of these pins."

"That's right. Gee, you got one of 'em in your hand. You suppose any were left out?"

A quiet, but often surly, mechanic named Evans had been in charge of these pins.

"Evans," said Lucky, "you sure you got all these things in right? If one was missing this crate would fly apart in a dive."

"Sure I got them in," growled Evans. "Check them if you don't believe it."

Lucky checked and found every bolt in place. Relieved, deciding the one he held had been the result of a miscount, he forgot about it.

He was far more interested in the conversation he had the next day with Commander Lawson.

"Hold everything," said Lucky. "We've finished the new dive bomber."

"Martin, I told you—" began Lawson.

"You will at least watch the test, won't you?"

The officer muttered about it for a while, finishing with, "To be frank with you, Martin, I don't believe you can make the cruise you said you could with it, even if it doesn't fly apart in the air. I'm not interested in seeing you killed, old man."

"Then supposing I put it this way," said Lucky. "I'll make

a cross-country trip first. Then if, under full load of guns and bombs, I fall down on you, we'll forget about it."

"As long as you've built it, name your date."

"Three weeks from today, weather permitting."

"All right," said Lawson. "It will at least prevent you from killing yourself. Three weeks from today."

CHAPTER FOUR

A First Test—and Bullets

T HIS is easy," said Lucky Martin when he landed at the
Naval Air Station.

"Prove it," said Lawson. "I've talked myself hoarse to the
powers and they've finally consented to give you an official
trial. It's eight o'clock. An observer is ready at Charleston,
South Carolina, which is, I believe, the required midway point."

"Right. I take off for Charleston at nine. At twelve-thirty
sharp I will be back here in Washington. Three and a half
hours, and no refueling in between."

"That's a big brag," smiled Lawson.

"Where's the armament, the bombs and whatever? Load,
my jolly tars!"

Flynn, who had been a half-winger in the long-forgotten
days along the Western Front, when Lucky Martin had been
building models, proudly took his position in the gunner's
cockpit and lorded over the mounting of the weapons.

Evans, who had come down from the factory with a truck,
disappeared for a few minutes, but Lucky did not give it a
second thought.

"All set?" said Lawson.

"On the line. See you at twelve-thirty."

"I hope so."

Lucky gunned the sleek, gleaming ship into the wind.

29

A sailor clicked a stopwatch and dropped his hand. The dive bomber leaped, quivering, down the field like mercury squirted from a tube.

Lucky gave himself over to the joy of speed and flight. Skimming the treetops, with the mighty engine thundering, he shot along the bank of the Anacostia River, down the Potomac, so low that his slipstream rippled the blurred water below.

He came up a little. White and green Mount Vernon, beaten by the engine's roar, was briefly under the stubby wings. Land again, flat plains, rickety houses.

The quicksilver javelin, fast as light, rolled back the screen of earth, devouring miles, throwing creeks and fields contemptuously behind.

Lucky knew what this plane would do. He knew what he could do. At twelve-thirty he would again be in Washington, DC.

The chronometer on the panel said ten-thirty when Charleston, white, lazy and blue, slid up over the curve of the world and fanned out under the streaking wings.

Flashing down the Battery, banking over Fort Sumter, he sliced a wide circle of blue, flirted his flippers at palms, bridges and mud flats, settled his black, spinning compass and roared north again.

A few miles north of Raleigh, North Carolina, just as they brushed the Roanoke River by, as one sweeps away a silver strand of spider web, Flynn's voice rang in the tube.

"A gray ship straight up!"

"As long as he keeps away—"

"He's got the height. He can dive."

Lucky squinted up through the glass dome of his shield. The gray ship, almost invisible against the dazzling sun, was starting down. Lucky knew he had the faster plane and he could not understand why anyone should want to intercept him. But the menace of the other plane, from a purely navigational point of view, was unmistakable.

"She's commercial," yelled Flynn.

"She's pursuit, but not service," corrected Lucky. "We'll show her our heels."

"She's got the speed out of that dive. For God's sake, zigzag!"

Lucky glanced up again and then down. The deserted hills of southern Virginia were under them. No witnesses down there.

"She's armed!" cried Flynn. "She's got two bow guns!"

"Are you loaded?"

"Yes."

"Remove your braces and set your sights. We'll rake this baby!"

Lucky touched rudder and eased back a little on the stick. The dive bomber needed no urging. It leaped skyward in a wingover, engine changing pitch like a siren.

For an instant, the two ships were head-on, and then Lucky dived out.

The .50-caliber machine gun quivered and flamed in Flynn's hands. He was warning the other plane off, shooting high.

The gray ship veered, spraying lead through its prop. All shots went wide.

Coming out of a loop, the gray ship, rolling, came out on the dive bomber's tail, guns stuttering above the cowl.

31

Lucky, facing his first aerial encounter, did the natural thing. He zoomed, for an instant almost motionless in the other's sights. Tracer drew a pattern of line just below the metal plane's tail.

Flynn was standing in the plunging pit, firing straight back, feeding bullets as big as his thumb through his racketing weapon.

The gray plane strove to dive out of range. The line of escape and the blue fingers of Flynn's tracer intersected. The blurred prop of the strange craft exploded into a fleeing squadron of splinters.

"Let me finish him off!" yowled Flynn into the tube.

"Haven't time!"

"Hell!"

The dive bomber verticaled back into its course.

Motorless, the gray ship was stabbing down at the flats below, a place of refuge in these rolling hills.

"Cold meat," mourned Flynn.

Lucky, mopping at his beaded brow, caught up on his breathing and settled his compass in the groove.

He had been ten minutes ahead of his time. The ten minutes were eaten up.

But before either of them had any time to brood on the matter, there was the Potomac again, the Anacostia and the Naval Air Station.

"Don't yip about that other ship," said Lucky.

"But gee whiz—"

"They'd think we were lying. We're on time and that's enough."

"Okay," sighed Flynn. "I go through the war without a score, and then when I get one, you won't let me talk about it. Hell of a life."

"There isn't any war, and we don't want to get into trouble."

Flynn's answer was drowned in the thump of the landing gear against the ground.

"Twelve-thirty," crowed Lucky, standing up in his pit.

Lawson grudgingly admitted that it was. The Charleston observer had radioed in the check.

"Now will you believe me?" said Lucky. "I tell you you can't get along without this sky devil. Tomorrow we give her the dives and sign the papers for a hundred."

"*If* she holds together," said Lawson.

"Oh," said Lucky, tempting his jinx beyond all endurance, "she'll hold together. Won't she, Dixie?"

"I . . . I hope so," said the girl who stood beside Lawson.

"If she don't," said Lucky, grinning, "you won't have enough left to bury me with. But then the Navy can do that. How about it, Lawson?"

Lawson shuddered. Strange people, these test pilots!

CHAPTER FIVE

Falling Wings and a Lost Ship

AS calm as though about to take a ride in a sightseeing bus, instead of a man-killing dive bomber, Lucky Martin hauled his helmet over his tousled brown hair and buckled the straps under his big chin.

"All through in a couple of hours," said Lucky, "and happy days are here again."

"You've got a tested chute?" said Dixie.

"Sure, but I won't need it."

"Don't tempt fate," pleaded Dixie, shivering although the day was warm. "You . . . you're all I've got now."

"You'll have a fortune to boot very shortly," grinned Lucky. "Did I ever let anybody down?"

"No."

"Then I never will. That little ship out there is as tough as a mustang, rarin' to go. Solid as the Rock of Gibraltar."

"I never—" said Dixie, feebly trying to cheer herself up by uttering an ancient aviation joke, "I never saw the Rock of Gibraltar in a power dive, so I don't know."

"Atta girl. Put on your earmuffs and keep the liniment handy for your neck. When I start down, you're going to see something!"

"I hope not. Lucky—"

"What?"

"Can't you ease her off at seven Gs? Can't you pull her punches a little?"

"The smoke meter in that crate won't lie and if she can't take it, we'll want to know before we start production."

"Then you'll try to pull her apart?"

"Sure I will, but she won't. Honey, that's my job. If they won't pull with me in the pit, they won't pull at all. Rough Rider, that's me. But if she does—"

"Then you think it might go to pieces . . . ?"

"No. It can't! There's the commander and the observers. Flynn! Rev her up, and let's have a listen at her."

Flynn, in the office, heeled the brakes and jabbed the throttle. The engine bellowed sweetly and then died off to a clicking murmur.

"Okay," said Flynn, surrendering his place and climbing down. "Give it hell, Lucky."

"All set," said Lawson.

Lucky reached out of the pit and gave Dixie's shoulder a reassuring shake. She managed a smile and he grinned back. Pulling the hood down over him, Lucky taxied into the wind, saluted the crowd, shoved upon throttle and stick and lanced down the runway and away from earth.

Evans, the mechanic, tried to look uninterested.

The dive bomber climbed as fast as a sixteen-inch shell—and fully as loud.

Anacostia tumbled away so quickly that it appeared in need of a chute. The Capitol and parks dwindled in size as though sprinkled with alum. The Washington Monument receded until it was nothing more than a toothpick stuck in a green carpet.

Bridges were black lines across the silver Potomac and the cars upon them were something less than moving periods.

To the south, Alexandria was enveloped in a haze. To the northeast, Baltimore was a black smudge. The rolling green of Maryland was laid out like a quilt, tacked to brown Virginia with blue tape.

Ten thousand, fifteen thousand, eighteen thousand.

Lucky went around three times, admiring the view through the glass of the hood, incidentally noting that the air was clear of ships under him.

He examined his neat cockpit, to make certain that everything was lashed down. That was necessary, because loose objects would float in front of his face when he started the dive.

For an instant he had an odd feeling in the region of his heart. A premonition reared black and ugly within him. He mopped at his face, although it was cold so high in the air.

What was the matter with him? He'd done this half a hundred times before. Wasn't he Lucky Martin? Other men might die, but hadn't he always pulled through? He knew his ship and he knew himself. Nothing could possibly happen. He knew exactly when to pull out. Even when the gravity gauge slid up to nine, even when the blood was driven down out of his head and everything went black, he knew what to do.

There was Bolling, there was the Naval Air Station. That was the target, he was the bullet.

"Fire, Gridley," muttered Lucky, trying to grin.

37

Back on the stick and throttle. Let her stall and whip out of it. He'd show them. Up came the nose. The ground was straight down at his back.

The dive bomber faltered, hung motionless for an instant, standing on its tail like a flying fish.

The bottom dropped out.

The nose swooped down with whip-crack speed. The earth tipped. The throttle shot up the trident.

With a bellow which made every window in Washington rattle and shake, the dive bomber started down.

Two-fifty, three hundred. Three-fifty, four hundred. Four-fifty . . . Terminal velocity!

The world was a monstrous cup. Everything was bowing back and up, except the green patch that was Bolling Field. That sank away, as though afraid of being hit by this rushing projectile.

Seven hundred feet per second, swifter than a small-bore bullet, the plane charged earthward.

Shaking, screaming, drumming at the faraway earth with its deafening thunder, the ship stayed in the perpendicular groove.

Swiftly the altimeter ran down its scale. Thirteen thousand, eleven, nine, six . . .

The time for the pullout was at hand. Would the plane hold together, or would it explode under the impact of air?

Time to pull out.

The hangars were getting larger and larger. The people increased from dots to white, strained faces. The river was stretching apart, getting wider and wider.

Five thousand, four . . .

The howling riot of the engine combined with the agonized shriek of the wires.

Three thousand!

Lucky came back a little on the stick. Too much would mean his instant death. Too much would slam an invisible ton weight upon him, squashing him into the seat.

The ship would take it. Still under control.

Back down and yell!

Lucky, to ease the piercing pain of his ears, roared unheard into the din and fought back the controls.

The earth whipped level with a mighty lurch. The plane streaked out in a horizontal line.

She was holding together!

Blood rushed from his head. Blackness shut down before Lucky's face. Before he had ended his shout, he was unconscious.

But this was always true. This was nothing to be concerned about. In an instant . . .

With a splintering crash, the wings burst apart. Sections dived to the right and left, to float in the blue.

Wingless, with nothing to stop it now, the dive bomber plummeted straight down, engine still yowling.

Lucky saw the wings. He felt the mighty jolt of their leaving. Stunned, but instantly alert, he unsnapped his belt and jabbed both hands against the glass hood which covered him.

Earth, people, river and blue sky all whirled in a mad cotillion.

The hood would not raise. He put his shoulders against it. Wind wrenched it out of his grasp and threw it up, tearing it from its hinges.

Windsock, trees, trucks, an already moving crash wagon . . .

Lucky managed to get his feet under him. He shoved himself halfway out of the pit. The savage slipstream almost ripped him in two, pinned him where he stood.

A boat on the Potomac, cars on the road, spinning lawns entangled with a glaring, cavorting sun . . .

Lucky was staring straight ahead, jaw set, strength useless against the sinews of the wind.

This instant he was alive. In the next he would be dead. But his whole being was concentrated on only one thing—the shock which would be Dixie O'Neal's. To see the plane and all her future destroyed in an instant, to see a cockpit bathed red with what remained of Lucky Martin . . .

A second is a century in the air.

Lucky lifted his foot and slammed it against the throttle. In the instant the projectile changed speed, inertia removed its clutching hand.

Flung out into the battering flow of air, turned over and over through lusting space, Lucky saw the earth three hundred feet under him.

His fingers gripped the rip cord and he started to pull. A wing fragment passed a yard from his head.

The pilot chute grabbed air and whistled back. The big chute cracked and flowed in a white bundle behind him, but not open.

He was still falling.

Flung out into the battering flow of air, turned over and over through lusting space, Lucky saw the earth three hundred feet under him.

One hundred, seventy-five, fifty . . . still falling free.

With a resounding slap, the main chute opened. The harness yanked him backward from the ground, bruising him.

An explosive crash to the right told him that the fuselage had hit in the open field.

Swaying gently like an acrobat on a trapeze, Lucky reached the earth and fought down the billowing chute which dragged at him.

He unbuckled his harness and when they reached him he was carefully wiping his face with a handkerchief.

"Got a smoke?" said Lucky to an awed sailor.

But everybody except Lucky was too excited to locate one.

Dixie's face was as pale as ice cream and she couldn't see because the world was swimming and misty. But she touched his sleeve to make sure that he was real.

"Have *you* got a smoke?" said Lucky.

Dixie opened her purse and handed him a pack and matches.

"There goes the old ball game," said Lucky, jerking his smoking cigarette at the smoking hole in the earth.

Lawson cleared his throat nervously. "Too bad and I won't say I told you so. I'll give you a report on this if you want, but all I can say is that the ship is only capable of usual wing loads and should not be recommended for anything but sporting use and private fliers who will give it no strain."

"I don't care about that. There's no decent market," said Lucky. "Who'd want a sporting plane of this design?"

"Well," said Lawson, "people do buy sporting planes. And just this morning Mr. Bullard was telling me that this crate, though useless to the government, might fill his needs. He has a foreign order for private planes, not of pursuit variety. This is the furthest thing from a fighting craft I ever saw, but it would fill a sporting requirement if equipped with a smaller engine. See Bullard. Don't give up."

"If you see him first," said Lucky, "tell him to go to the devil. I don't like him. This is a dive bomber—or was."

"It is and was a pile of junk," said Lawson, stiffly. "A sport plane and nothing more. See Bullard."

"Nuts," said Lucky Martin, taking Dixie's arm. "Let's go."

CHAPTER SIX

The Devil Springs a Trap

DIXIE mysteriously produced ten dollars and Flynn, sworn to secrecy, did not reveal that he had hocked her wristwatch worth a hundred and fifty.

And thus it was that they ate for three days.

At the end of that time the wires Lucky Martin had sent (collect) were answered severally to the effect that it was vacation time as far as test pilots were concerned.

"I guess," said Lucky, sitting on the porch of the soon-to-be-foreclosed O'Neal mansion, "that I'd better contact an airline."

"I did this morning," said Dixie. "I called up the general manager of EAT, and he says he has a waiting list as long as a Department of Commerce appropriation bill."

"Maybe Western Air—"

"Plans," said Dixie, "are fine as long as they remain in the dream stage. But I was wrong."

"I'm not licked yet," said Lucky in a hopeless tone of voice.

"Of course not."

"We'll . . . we'll . . . Well, what the hell will we do?"

"The plant is going to go under the hammer, and everything else as well. But never mind, Lucky. I studied bookkeeping and I—"

"Nix. We're not that low . . . or are we? Say, when did this street allow dirigible traffic?"

The object of his remark, trailed by sallow and shambling Smith, came up the walk.

"Nice afternoon," replied Bullard.

"It *was*," said Lucky.

"Mind if I sit down?" said Bullard.

"Sure, if that chair can take it."

"You're not very cordial," said Bullard, gently reproving, after the fashion of a rhinoceros.

"You ought to be a mind reader," said Lucky. "Dixie, I think you had better go in. I'm about to tell this Bullard what I think of him."

Dixie stayed where she was.

Bullard, seated in the creaking chair, smiled in a bland good humor. "So I ought to be a mind reader. All right, Lucky Martin. I'll start now. Your government threw you down twice, I catch you on the bounce. Mr. Smith, here, has kindly consented to give you another chance. You are at present thinking about how broke you are, how futile it is to try and find a decent job, and you're wondering when you'll next eat. Five million dollars—"

"I said no once. I don't often change my mind."

"Stubborn men seldom do," replied Bullard. "But I have something that might change it."

"I doubt that."

Bullard pulled a bolt from his vest pocket and tossed it up, catching it in his fat hand. "You see this?"

"It's a wing pin."

46

"That's right," said Bullard. "It seems to be a perfectly good bolt, doesn't it?"

"What of it?"

"It's not, that's all. It's not steel, it's bad wrought iron."

"Well?"

"You wouldn't want to be hanged for the murder of Big Tom O'Neal, would you, Martin?"

Lucky stood up and casually examined his fist. "You can leave any time you want, Bullard."

The personification of a balloon did not stir.

"Smith," said Bullard, "call for Evans."

Smith called, and in a moment, Evans sullenly shuffled up the steps and stood uneasily, avoiding Martin's eyes.

"Evans," said Bullard, "you work at the O'Neal plant."

"He did, but he was just fired," said Lucky.

"Evans," continued Bullard with judicial inflexion, "have you ever seen a bolt like this before?"

"Yeah."

"Where?"

"In Mr. Martin's hand at the plant."

"And what was Martin doing with this bolt?"

"He . . . he was changing it for a solid steel pin the night before O'Neal got washed out."

"And you are ready to swear to that?"

"Yeah."

"Very good, Evans," said Bullard, "you can wait at the car."

"You bet," said Lucky, and before anyone else could move, Lucky seized Evans by the arm and threw him down the steps and into a rosebush.

47

"I'll get you for that!" squealed Evans, tangled up with thorns.

Lucky was down the steps before the words were fully uttered. He snatched Evans up, though the man was not a weakling, and with a well-placed right, knocked him down again.

A kick catapulted Evans on his way, and Lucky, his hair in his eyes and his fists as big and hard as grenades—and quite as ready to explode—went for Bullard.

Smith was standing to one side, a shaky automatic in his bony fingers. "Stay where you are!"

Bullard stood up and his right hand bulged in his coat pocket. "Come up and sit down, Mr. Martin. We want to talk with you."

Lucky, even then, would have charged them both. But with a chilled heart he saw that Bullard's hidden weapon was pointed at Dixie.

Forced into a chair, Lucky restlessly tried to think of a way out.

"We've got you for murder," said Bullard. "You bumped old man O'Neal to get the plant. Your own men heard you quarreling with him just before he took that flight. So did the people on the field. We preserved the wreckage for examination and three bad pins are still in it, and two are in a wing section I picked up after it broke. These pins—"

"You're lying!" cried Dixie.

"The courts won't think so. I've got witnesses, I've got the evidence—"

"You caused that crash in Washington!" said Lucky.

"They'll find nothing in the wreck but good pins . . . *now*," grinned Bullard. "No, my fine murderer, there is no way out."

"Lucky! He can't do it!" wailed Dixie.

"I can," said Bullard. "And, what's more to the point, I will. Unless, of course, you listen to reason."

"That's blackmail!" said Lucky.

"Bright boy," said Bullard.

"Go to the cops," said Lucky. "Tell them your lies, produce your perjured witnesses, and see how far you get!"

"I'll get far enough to see you hanged," replied Bullard.

"I won't go through with it! I refuse to violate the Neutrality Laws!"

Bullard grinned fatly. "Who said anything about violating any laws?"

"But if you manufacture fighting planes at the O'Neal plant and then export them, the United States will stop you in your tracks. I don't care what blind you use, it can't be done! Do you think the Army spends its time playing tiddlywinks? Do you think the Navy sails its boats in a bathtub? And what about the agents of the Treasury Department, the Coast Guard? Bullard, you're insane. You can't get away with this thing. You might be able to force me to build the planes, but you'll never get those same ships beyond the three-mile limit!"

Bullard lighted up a cigar and gazed at Lucky pityingly. "My boy, you lack finesse. You may be a fine test pilot but you will never make a diplomat. Have I said anything about your building *dive bombers* for my client? No. Why, you call me insane without knowing any of the facts."

"I know enough of them," snapped Lucky. "Three years ago half a dozen pilots tried to get away with this. They got caught in Peru and the US wrecked them for life. One shipment of fighting planes went out to Spain because Congress was slow getting the law through, but none have gone since. I know that China is yowling for US fighting ships. I know that Outer Mongolian warlords will pay anything for them. Take your client British planes, French planes, any planes, but, Bullard, you'll never get so much as a joystick out of the territorial limits of the United States. The sooner you get that through your head, the better off you'll be. *Nobody* can do such a thing with the United States as alert to such a move as it has lately become. Put that in your cigar and blow it up."

Bullard was still grinning. "England, you say? France, Italy . . . ? Lucky Martin, you must know that all of those places are using every available factory and every available ship in the present arms race. The *only* place in the world I can get these ships is right here in the USA. And, Martin, you're going to build them for me."

"But, damn it, I tell you you're a fool. You'll never get them out!"

"Do you think that shipload to which you refer," said Bullard, "would have risked possible confiscation if the reward at the other end had not been enormous? No. You underrate me, test pilot. If you think I am such a fool, I do not blame you for turning down my offer."

Bullard looked about him carefully. He was evidently very sure that Lucky could not use the information he was about to impart.

Bullard hitched forward with a confidential air. "See here, does the new law say anything about private planes? Sporting planes?"

"No," said Lucky, dubiously.

"You know definitely," said Bullard, "that the private plane manufacturers sell a large percent of their goods to a foreign market."

"Yes," said Lucky, uncomfortably.

"Your dive bomber," said Bullard, "is remarkable for its easy handling and its enormous horsepower. Did you think I needed your engines? No, we have better engines abroad. Did you think I needed your bomb-rack type? No, any outfit can duplicate them."

"What the hell do you want then?"

"You have developed a new wing design which should stand terrific pressure. It will with good wing pins. You have developed a new alloy for lightness. You have a new type of cockpit design. There you have it, Martin."

"I still don't see," said Lucky. "You can't possibly get past every arm of the government."

"You forget," said Bullard, puffing contentedly upon his cigar, "that you have twice pulled off your wings before official observers, doubly proving your wing design to be no good whatever. You forget that the government has twice turned you down. You forget that Commander Lawson turned in a report to the effect that this type of wing will apparently serve only in a sporting capacity."

"Where does all this lead?" cried Dixie, feeling that Lucky was being trapped.

"It leads, fair lady," said Bullard, "to nothing more and nothing less than this."

He fumbled in his capacious pockets and finally brought forth an official-looking letter to which was appended a permit.

"Read there," said Bullard, "that I am authorized to construct, for export, one hundred sporting planes. Read there that the wing load and stress is to be far less than that required for any fighting plane. The top speed is to be one hundred and ten miles per hour. The horsepower is not to be more than one hundred and twenty-five. This will apply to all ships save one, which will be equipped, unlike the rest, with mounts, bomb racks, and your regular engine."

"The government issued you this?" said Lucky with a frown.

"I have friends," said Bullard. "The failure of your bomber for fighting purposes aided my effort to have this permit issued."

"But if Lawson gets wind of that one ship," cried Lucky, thinking he saw a way out, "he'll queer your whole deal."

"Lawson already knows it will be built," said Bullard. "I told him you would not consent to building these sporting ships unless I allowed you to construct one last plane for testing. And this one last ship will never leave the United States!"

"But, damn it," said Lucky, "these sporting planes are of no concern to the government. They are no menace to anything. Why do you come like this to me?"

Bullard smiled. "I was afraid you wouldn't see light otherwise. You do not seem to like me, Martin."

"There's something behind this," snapped Lucky. "You

STORIES from the GOLDEN AGE

☐ Yes, I would like to receive my **FREE CATALOG** featuring all 80 volumes of the *Stories from the Golden Age Collection* and more!

Name

Shipping Address

City   State   ZIP

Telephone   E-mail

Check other genres you are interested in: ☐ SciFi/Fantasy ☐ Western ☐ Mystery

FREE SHIPPING!
NO PURCHASE REQUIRED

6 Books • 8 Stories
Illustrations • Glossaries

6 Audiobooks • 12 CDs
8 Stories • Full color 40-page booklet

- -
Fold on line and tape

IF YOU ENJOYED READING THIS BOOK, GET THE ACTION/ADVENTURE COLLECTION AND SAVE 25%

BOOK SET	**AUDIOBOOK SET**
$59.50 $45.00	$77.50 $58.00
ISBN: 978-1-61986-089-6	ISBN: 978-1-61986-090-2

☐ Check here if shipping address is same as billing.

Name

Billing Address

City   State   ZIP

Telephone   E-mail

Credit/Debit Card #: _____

Card ID # (last 3 or 4 digits): _____

Exp Date: _____/_____ Date (month/day/year): _____/_____/_____

Order Total *(CA and FL residents add sales tax)*: _____

To order online, go to: **www.GoldenAgeStories.com** or call toll-free **1-877-8GALAXY** or 1-323-466-7815

© 2012 Galaxy Press, LLC. All Rights Reserved. Pulp magazines cover artwork is reprinted with permission from Argosy Communications, Inc.; Penny Publications, LLC; Hachette Filipacchi Media; and Condé Nast Publications.

NO POSTAGE
NECESSARY
IF MAILED
IN THE
UNITED STATES

BUSINESS REPLY MAIL
FIRST-CLASS MAIL   PERMIT NO. 75738   LOS ANGELES CA

POSTAGE WILL BE PAID BY ADDRESSEE

GALAXY PRESS
7051 HOLLYWOOD BLVD
LOS ANGELES CA   90028-9771

STORIES from the GOLDEN AGE
by L. Ron Hubbard

COLLECT THEM ALL!

GALAXY
PRESS

7051 Hollywood Blvd., Suite 200 • Hollywood, CA 90028
1-877-8GALAXY or 1-323-466-7815
To sign up online, go to:
www.GoldenAgeStories.com

Prices set in US dollars only. Non-US residents, please call 1-323-466-7815 for pricing information or go to www.GoldenAgeStories.com.
Sales tax where applicable. Terms, prices and conditions subject to change.

haven't a market for a hundred sport planes flying a hundred and ten an hour."

"By my papers," said Bullard, "it has been proved to the government that I have."

"But there's no point in going to all this trouble just to get ships for private aviation."

"Only you and I," said Bullard, "will know that the first two dive bombers folded up in the air because of faulty wing pins."

A bright light broke upon Lucky, almost stunning him with its brilliance. Smooth, plausible Bullard had a permit straight from the government to have O'Neal Aircraft construct a hundred slow-flying, innocuous ships using the O'Neal wing design and fuselage—both of which had been proved worthless by actual test for fighting purposes.

But only Bullard and Dixie and Lucky Martin knew that the wing design was correct. On the other side of the world, Bullard would shift the engines for more powerful plants, would carve out the bellies and fit in bomb racks, and there he would have the most potent light bomber ever manufactured.

Lucky could not blame blind Lawson. Even if Lucky managed to get word to the government, they would call him a liar and laugh at him. Under no charge whatever could Bullard be brought to account.

What was wrong with exporting a private plane which had been tested and found to be worthless as a fighting ship? What was wrong with manufacturing them?

A man with less nice ethics than Lucky Martin would

have gladly gone ahead with the deal. But Lucky knew his government was wrong, knew that the ship *was* a potential menace as a bomber.

"No. I can't do it," said Lucky.

"Then I am prepared to make matters difficult for you, Martin," said Bullard." I supposed you would be stubborn about this. I am okay with the government, with everybody, and I'm going to be okay with you. You think quite a lot of this young lady—"

"Lucky," cried Dixie, "you won't—"

"If he doesn't," said Bullard, licking his lips, "I wouldn't give ten cents Mex for your looks and life, young lady. Smith, call the boys!"

Presently three men swaggered into sight and up the steps. One of them, addressed as Two-Finger, wore a checkered cap pulled low over his coarse face. The other two, common as the refuse in the gutter, stood insolently eyeing Dixie O'Neal.

"See this girl?" said Bullard.

"Good looking," commented the man.

"You are to guard her closely. She is not to speak to any persons unknown to you. She is not to go near a phone. She is to stay either here or at the plant. But understand this. You are not to harm her as long as Lucky Martin behaves. Is that clear?"

"You're clear as corn liquor, gov'ner," said Two-Finger.

"And you two," said Bullard to the unsavory pair, "are to stay with Martin wherever he goes, hear everything he says, and report instantly to Two-Finger if Martin fails to work, or if he oversteps his liberty. In that event, you know what to do with him. Understand?"

They nodded.

"And now," said Bullard to Lucky, "shall we go inside and arrange our plans for the production of a hundred *private sport planes*?"

"Bullard," said Lucky, "I'll promise nothing. It seems to me that a certain giant bomber crashed twice recently and you couldn't work the deal there. You've used pull and dollars to get by here, but I'm telling you that if there's anything I can do to trip you up—"

"The planes will be all right. I told you we'd build one dive bomber. I also told Lawson that I was letting you do it, and he shook his head and said you were crazy, that the crate was no good. But that one dive bomber will be selected from all the planes. *And you'll test it*, Unlucky Martin."

CHAPTER SEVEN

Lucky, the Laughingstock—

WEARY weeks later, Dixie, under unsuitable escort, made one of her infrequent visits to the plant. While Two-Finger puffed a cigar under a No-Smoking sign, and while the other two guards lounged nearby eyeing Lucky, a limited conversation was possible.

"Benedict Arnold did something like this one," grimaced Lucky.

"Don't look at it that way," said Dixie. "You've been forced by circumstances—"

"So was Mr. Arnold, but that didn't make less a traitor out of him."

"But nothing bad will come of this. A hundred sport planes wouldn't wreck anything."

"A hundred dive bombers could sink a navy," said Lucky.

"But if the government says your ships are no good—"

"You and I and this Bullard know they're all right. And worst of all, *I* know it. Just because two crashed . . . Say, there's that aircraft inspector again."

Dixie looked quickly at the hangar door and saw a small, unimposing man step inside. Not in the least worried, Bullard stood in the office door and called a greeting to him.

The inspector smiled and approached Lucky. "Things are looking up for you, Martin."

"Yeah," said Lucky in a sour voice.

"Glad all your tests didn't add up to a total loss, anyhow," said the inspector. "Sport planes are cheaper, but better than nothing. Put you on your feet again, anyway."

Risking later thunder and lightning from Bullard, Lucky said, "If some people weren't so dumb, they'd know they were *still* dive bombers."

Bullard looked quite unworried.

The inspector smiled. "Still sticking to it, eh? Lawson was around the other day and he said you were just about the most stubborn guy in the business. Why do you keep worrying about a ship after it's gone bad twice?"

"With a bigger engine and bomb racks," said Lucky, "they're good dive bombers."

"Sure," said Bullard indulgently. "Have a cigar, Inspector?"

"We better smoke outside, unless you want this place to burn down on you," said the inspector. "Still anxious to try another ship as a dive bomber, Martin?"

"Be on hand and you'll see," said Lucky.

The inspector grinned and shook his head. "I don't like to watch guys kill themselves, thank you. How's everything going along, Bullard?"

A moment later Bullard was back. But he was no longer pleasant. "Trying to tip him off, are you?" he roared.

"Somebody will have to," said Lucky. "They won't believe me."

"Of course they won't, after what I've been feeding them about you. You Two-Finger! Get on the job and get this dame out of here."

Two-Finger looked sad. "I can't do nothin' with her, boss. All I can do is keep her away from people. I . . . I've been having to spend nights sittin' on her front steps, and it ain't hot out neither. I got a breakdown comin' on. See that red streak on my jaw? She gimme that for trying to go inside one night it rained."

Dixie stepped gingerly past Bullard, walking like a well-bred Persian anxious to avoid contact with garbage. Her roadster, now out of hock as well as her other possessions, was now waiting for her on the tarmac. Two-Finger tried to slide into the front seat but Dixie gave him a stormy rake of canister with her eyes and Two-Finger, cowed, slunk into the rumble.

"You try that again," said Bullard, when only dust remained to mark the place the roadster had stood, "and you'll see something that will amaze you. You got any idea which of these planes I mean to make up as a dive bomber?

"No, and you won't have until the last minute. Therefore, Unlucky Martin, you'd better be sure they're all okay, each and every one. You're going to test one of these through all its paces, see?"

Bullard went away, and Flynn, who was busy hoisting one of the small engines into its mount, spat brownly upon the place where Bullard had stood.

"You better watch it," said Flynn, lowering his voice so the other mechanics and the guards could not hear. "I was down in the locker yesterday and I heard this Smith and Bullard talking via the ventilator. They'll make one real dive bomber all right and you'll test it. Smith, who's got a pursuit ship

59

parked south of here in an old barn, is to go with you. You get slugs in the back of your head, the dive bomber crashes as further proof to the government that it ain't any good. Smith meets Bullard at sea."

Lucky, testing the balance of a prop, pretended not to hear.

"Bullard," continued Flynn, "has taken a likin' to Dixie and she's not going to be left behind when they leave. As you'll carry a load of bombs in your tests, you'll be splattered all over the landscape when you crash and there's no evidence. I get shanghaied to replace these small engines with big power plants and bomb racks. Nobody is left to breathe a word about what's happened."

Lucky went on working as though he had heard nothing. But he felt sick. Everyone had turned against him except Flynn and Dixie. He and the dive bomber were the laughingstock of the government. His death would occasion no surprise, as the news had been carefully prepared far in advance. The dive bomber, branded as worthless, might someday be used to destroy battleships flying the American flag.

He knew why he had to die. If he ever lived to finance the construction of yet another dive bomber, he could test it and prove once and for all that it would do all he said it would. And if that happened, Bullard would be sought for the way he had managed this mammoth hoax.

Lucky watched Smith and wondered how it would feel to have your head blown off with a .50-caliber machine gun. Lucky watched Bullard and remembered that incendiary ammunition did well in blowing up balloons.

And ship by ship, the *private sport planes* were taken away to be loaded openly upon a freighter. Day by day the time of the final test approached.

CHAPTER EIGHT

She Stays Together— So What?

BULLARD had done his work so well that when the day came to ask the Department of Commerce for an Experimental X license, the inspector balked. And Lawson, at his side, chorused his doubt.

"I can't let Martin kill himself," explained the inspector.

"It's suicide," Commander Lawson said to Bullard. "I've seen the plane crash twice and I came down here the moment I heard about it to forbid the issuance of a license if I could."

"Now, gentlemen," said the suave Bullard, glancing at Lucky, "you know how the boy has been yapping. He thinks his ship will stand the dive this time and, as part of his pay, I let him equip one for military purposes. Now we all know it will crash, but we can't refuse Lucky Martin his chance, can we?"

"I won't attend any test," vowed Lawson. "I won't watch him pull another one apart. It's too hard on the nerves. We have already declared that it is only good for *sporting* purposes and we can't change our minds now."

"Please, gentlemen," said Bullard. "You can't do this to Martin."

"Commander," said Lucky, "if this one stays in one piece, won't that indicate that these export ships could all be converted into dive bombers at their destination?"

It was a bold stroke, and though Bullard, could have struck Lucky dead where he stood from rage, Bullard had to smile.

"Two crashes were enough," said Lawson. "You're a stubborn fool, Martin."

"I have no real grounds on which to base a refusal to issue this Experimental," said the inspector doubtfully.

"Of course you haven't," said Bullard. "We must give the boy his chance."

"I refuse to attend such nonsense," said Lawson. With a scowl he marched out of the plant, got into his car and drove away.

With Lawson out of the road, Bullard made fast work of the inspector, and the X was granted on Bullard's affidavit that the plane had been improved.

And then, because he did not think the plane would be ready to test that day, the inspector also departed, taking Lucky's last hope with him.

Neither Dixie nor Flynn were in sight. But Smith was there, battening a .50-caliber machine gun to his ring mount.

The test was evidently not to be conducted over the O'Neal plant and the plane was flown by Smith to a field some distance away.

Bullard took Lucky with him in his car, guards close at hand, and after a long drive, they came to a wide field in the country. Smith was already waiting for them.

Lucky wondered just how this would be done, just when he would get his. On this test dive, or on the following cross-country trip?

Shaky and jittery Smith might appear, but for all that, there was nothing wrong with his nerves. Coolly he buckled his seat pack and crawled in. The gun occasioned no comment because the plane had to be tested under a full military load.

Lucky looked at the empty bomb racks. "She hasn't got all her weight with her."

Bullard's confidence in Smith's ability was amazing. "Fill the racks," he ordered.

Streamlined bombs were clamped into the compartments. Lucky, satisfied, stepped into his cockpit and strapped his helmet down. He felt very lonely. He could not remember a time when Dixie had been absent at a test takeoff. He missed her smile, her advice for caution, her pretense at being calm.

"Get going," said Smith in his whiney voice. But there was no mistaking the command in his black diamond eyes.

Lucky pulled down his hood without looking back. He jabbed throttle.

The bordering trees fled in a blur. The wheels lightened and parted from the earth. Lucky cranked the gear into the belly of the ship, let up the wing flaps, adjusted the tab trim with expert fingers.

Reckless, half hoping for disaster, he stood the ship on its tail and shot it at the zenith, engine full on and clamouring a protest against such violence.

"Take it easy," said Smith into the tube. Lucky noted that the voice was not in the least afraid. Another stick was back there, all connected.

The dive bomber went up the scale like a spurred Pegasus. The altimeter lifted visibly without pause. Ten, twelve, fourteen thousand feet.

"Pull out at eight thousand, when you dive," said Smith.

Minutes passed, the altimeter touched the big white twenty. Lucky leveled off and looked over the side.

Even the bulk of Bullard was invisible on the green, yellow and brown chessboard below. The world curved off to its horizons, a crisscross of white lines which were rivers and highways.

"Get it over with," ordered Smith.

Lucky went into a dive so fast that his inertia pulled him clear of the seat. Full throttle, accelerating ten times as fast as a freely falling body, streaking in a vertical line, the diminutive bomber eagerly devoured great gulps of the four miles down.

A red barn, a big barn about the size of a match head, was Lucky's target. The eaves fanned out, the yard became square, the wind vane's movements on the peak grew plain.

"Eight thousand!" screamed Smith into the racketing yowl of engines and wings.

They were past terminal velocity, lancing into a blurred funnel of swelling earth.

The altimeter was at the big white eight.

Lucky jockeyed his stick. The fins were biting.

"Out!" yelled Lucky and instantly followed with a wild shout. Back on the stick.

A sledgehammer hit the underside of the ship, almost halting it in midair.

Abruptly the earth dropped flat and tipped to normal level.

The dive bomber, streaking straight ahead at something more than four hundred miles an hour, had held!

For a moment Lucky Martin exulted in the ship. She was perfect. Full load of bombs. Two men. And not even a quiver as it came out. A perfect plane!

Let the clumsy, waddling battleships beware when the O'Neal bomber took the skies. No gun could get into position fast enough to stop that terrific dive. Nothing could stop the imminent hail of bombs, themselves carried by a swift projectile. Nothing could disturb the gunner's aim when he laid the eggs on a rolling deck, because the plane itself decreed the path of the missiles . . .

Suddenly, as they slowed to cruising, the taste of triumph was as stale as cigarette ashes in his mouth.

Who knew but that those battleship targets might someday be flying the Stars and Stripes?

Listlessly, flying as mechanically as a robot, Lucky cut the gun and slid earthward on dismal, moaning wings.

He let down the wheels and floated until they caressed the earth.

"She stayed together," said Smith to Bullard, just as though Bullard had been in China during the dive.

"Of course she did. The pins were sound this time," said Bullard. "Okay, Martin, hop her back to the plant field. I'll meet you there."

Smith still stayed in the pit and Lucky, feeling worse than ever, again took off and clipped hedges on his way back.

Dixie was on the tarmac and, inevitably, Two-Finger was puffing a cigar at a respectful distance. Lucky's pair of leeches immediately fastened themselves to him.

"It worked," said Lucky.

"Then it's a success after all!" cried Dixie, forgetfully happy about it.

"Yes, damn the luck. I could sell them to the Navy in spite of what Lawson says. He couldn't afford to overlook them."

"Oh, Lucky, if you could just afford to tell him about those wing pins . . . But Lucky! It's not too late. They said they'd give you money. All you have to do is build another after they leave—"

"Yeah?" said Bullard, getting out of his car. "That's okay by me, Martin." The fat wrinkles about his eyes almost hid the amused brilliance of the unsavory orbs.

"You said you'd give me the dough," said Lucky. "My job is finished. All you have to do is load the rest of these crated ships and deliver them to collect yours."

"Oh, so you want the money," said Bullard. "Well, Martin, in spite of what you think, I'm a pretty good fellow after all. I'll make that three hundred thousand bucks, and I've got them right here."

He produced them, a staggering number of thousand-dollar bills—but he did not hand them over.

"Before we go into this," Bullard said, "you still have to test the cross-country ability to make it official. I'll want to know if I need any more of your engineering advice and if we have to make any changes before we ship. I'll put these bills in your safe, just to make sure you get them and I'll send Smith with you to see that you don't run off. Is that clear?"

Flynn, in the doorway, stabbed a warning glance at Lucky.

"That's clear," said Lucky, ambiguously.

"All right, you," said Bullard, indicating Flynn. "Fill this crate's tanks to the brim, see she's got plenty of oil, and take a listen at her engine. You'll have a fine flight, Martin."

"Will you be gone long?" said Dixie.

"It all depends," said Bullard.

"Yeah," muttered Flynn, nursing a gas hose, "it all depends!"

CHAPTER NINE

With a Machine Gun at His Head

THE sensations of a man who knows definitely that he is to be shot in the back of the head are not nearly as acute as those of a man who is in doubt as to both the deed and the time it will be performed.

In the latter case there is still hope of salvation, in the former there is only fatalistic resignation. According to Sing Sing guards, members of firing squads both Chinese and Russian, and the accounts of executioners, a condemned man is docile only when he knows definitely that there is no chance of being spared.

Darting south at six miles a minute, four thousand feet up, presumably testing the cruising range of the ship at full throttle, Lucky Martin, the man who always rode the skies with death's scythe an ever-present shadow in the clear blue about him, rode now with a jittery skeleton of a man less than four feet behind him, a man who held the butt of a machine gun throwing slugs the size of a pecan with enough power to somersault an elephant.

Desolate, rolling, brown hills were stretched below the scudding belly of the dive bomber. Spring had not yet brought its green to southern Virginia.

A good place for it, if it was to happen.

Lucky could not help glancing back every fifteen seconds. Cased like a mummy in a glass coffin, Smith gave him stare for stare. It was not necessary to remove the hood to fire the mounted gun. Lucky had his engineering skill to thank for that.

It was impossible to reach out of his own cage and get at the man. Smith would, of course, shoot away Lucky's hood as well as his head and drop the corpse into a sluggish river.

It was near this place that Lucky and Flynn had been attacked by the gray pursuit ship.

The long, flared snout of the gun pointed forward and up, which was as it should be. But when the bomber jarred into an infrequent bump, the snout wavered—which was not as it should be, because it meant that Smith held the butt, instead of keeping it lashed down.

The muzzle came down. Lucky caught the shadow of it on his shoulder.

He sensed that Smith already held the controls.

Lucky had set the tab-trimming control. The plane would stay in level flight with or without guidance.

He knew he would not go out passively, shot in the back.

With a lunge, he slammed his shoulders against his hood, knocking it open. In the same motion he unsnapped his belt and whirled to his knees in the seat, facing Smith.

The machine gun was aimed. Lucky grabbed at the muzzle.

Smith's eyes dilated like a cat's. His hand snatched the triggers.

The gun would not move in Lucky's grip! He was staring down its black tunnel.

A roar shook the plane as a shell went off.

Lucky flinched.

The slipstream battered him. The bomber started to climb.

Dazed with disbelief, Lucky saw coils of blue smoke oozing out of the gunner's pit. Smith's bloody right hand was pounding at the action.

Lucky, staking everything on one last try, amazed that he could still move, jabbed his fingers under the rear cockpit's hood and shoved it back in its groove.

Smith left the gun and strove to get a revolver out of his coat.

Like an avenging angel in a power dive, Lucky swooped down on Smith.

Precarious as his position was, he held to his cockpit with his heels over the dizzy earth, and hauled the struggling Smith clear of the belt and gun and seat.

Smith's screams went unheard. Lucky knocked his holds loose. With the finality of a steam shovel, Lucky handed Smith to the blast of chilly air.

Smith, sliding backward, hit an elevator fin as he fell. The bomber lurched drunkenly. Smith went spinning away with four thousand feet under him, growing smaller and smaller against the diminutive dun landscape.

But Smith still had his luck and he still had his chute and presently the canopy of white silk cracked open and hid him from view.

Lucky got back into his own pit with difficulty. The plane was trying to fall off into a spin, the maimed fin dragging. Barely able to keep on an even keel, Lucky had no time to watch Smith. He could not turn. He had to fly straight ahead, or get into a fatal bank.

Somewhere on his course he would find a field—he hoped.

Skidding, yawing, diving and then zooming, the bomber carved an erratic path along the sky.

Three miles ahead lay a clearing which looked big enough for the hard task of bringing this locoed Pegasus to earth.

He kissed the tops of trees, flirted with a fence, and finally, after nervous wooing, came secure to the soft bosom of the earth.

Shaking with reaction, remembering now that it had been very dangerous, Lucky climbed down.

A glance at the machine gun showed that it had exploded its breech. Just why that was, Lucky could not immediately find. But a few minutes of probing into the maimed metal disclosed that a wing bolt, its end filed off, had been driven forcibly into the breech end of the barrel.

Lucky mopped his face again. Good old Flynn had done that. He had fixed it while he was making his inspection, as per Bullard's orders.

A gentleman who chewed tobacco and, rather unnecessarily, smoked a pipe as well, shuffled along the furrows, looked intently at the bomber and finally, after spitting a couple quarts of brown juice, remarked, "It's an airplane."

"Right. Where's the nearest machine shop?" demanded Lucky.

"Well, now, let me see. If yuh go to Jackson, it'll take a long time, but if you goes to Beauregard, you'll find it closer."

"Is there a machinist in Beauregard?"

"No, can't say as there is."

"Damn it man, I've got to get this repaired right away!"

Lucky, recalling the rest of Flynn intelligence about the scheme, knew that an hour's delay might prove fatal to Dixie.

"Looks like you hit somethin' with it, suh."

"I ran into an air bump. I've got to get to a machine shop. Is there one in Jackson?"

"No, don't think so. Roanoke is over there about sixty miles, and Richmond is up that way, but you couldn't get it done today. Be dark before you got there."

The gentleman loafed along the fuselage and took hold of the broken fin and shook it leisurely, as though shaking hands with the plane.

"I've got to get it fixed!" wailed Lucky.

"Well, now, a piece of tin might patch it all right, if a feller had a piece of tin. I reckon—"

"Sure it would!" cried Lucky. "I've got to get out of here. Isn't there a machinist close by?"

"Well, I reckon there is."

"Where?"

"Well, I'm a pretty good machinist. I got a shop on the farm, over there a piece. If you could run this thing . . ."

Lucky was already in the pit, taxiing the ship. He got as close to the sheds as the fences would allow, and the machinist went to work with thoroughness if not speed.

Fuming and consuming whole smoke screens of cigarettes, Lucky watched the work go slowly forward. At last, satisfied that the task would not be done before dark and that he could not depart before the first grayness of dawn, he walked up a road and found a telephone line and pursued it to a connection in a general store.

Remembering that Smith had probably been the pilot of the gray ship, and that the gray ship was somewhere near at hand, and supposing that Smith would find it before night, he started to call Washington.

But with the number already given, he stepped back and hung up.

He could not do this until he was certain that Dixie was safe. Any hint of official interference—and he could not trust to governmental speed—would immediately seal Dixie's fate. Chances were that she would not be near the plant, but at her home, with Two-Finger close at hand. And he could not even guarantee that he would find her at her house.

Dolefully he trudged back down the road to the toiling farmer.

"Be done about noon tomorrow," said the machinist-elect.

"What's the delay now?"

"Why, there ain't a bolt the right size on the place, and I'll have to run them down from Jackson first thing in the morning."

Lucky sank weakly down on a rail and stared dismally at the empty, twilight sky.

The Takeoff for Trouble!

IT was one o'clock before Lucky could take off. It was two-twenty-five when he flashed down out of the sky upon the O'Neal plant.

He spent a very few seconds looking down at the doll-size buildings because they were obviously deserted. Neither smoke nor dust stirred in the listless breeze.

The dive bomber yawed to a stop before the tarmac and Lucky lit running. The outer door was locked but his shoulder remedied that. Catapulted into the gloom, he came to a startled stand before the blasted safe.

No money in there or anything else. No plans, no papers.

He heard footsteps outside and spun about to face the door. Flynn limped through the opening.

Flynn's face was bruised and bloody. He was covered with mud and his clothing was torn.

"God, I'm glad to see you, Lucky."

"What's happened to you?"

"Those two bulldogs that was guarding you started to guard me. I managed to knock one out and get his gun and kill the other one. I got away, but I was too late."

"Where's Dixie?"

"Halfway to Europe by this time."

"But . . . but that steamer couldn't have gotten out of the Chesapeake so quick! It must be close to Hampton Roads."

"No," said Flynn, passing a shaky hand carefully over a black eye. "That ship left here three days ago. Bullard grabbed Dixie right after you left. Ninety-nine planes are aboard the steamer. Smith was to blast you, make you crash, get his own plane in the south and meet the steamer at sea. Bullard and the others caught the boat at Norfolk, and they're halfway to Europe by now."

"We've got to do something!" wailed Lucky. He grabbed the phone and begged for the Treasury Department and the Coast Guard. He rapidly told them the details about the dive bomber, but the Coast Guard knew all about Bullard, his export permit, the planes. They also had been carefully coached about Lucky Martin. The answer was, "Sorry, Mr. Martin, I am afraid you are a little excited." Lucky thought wildly for an instant and then remembered that the steamer was registered under the US flag, that Dixie would be an excuse for the Coast Guard. Rapidly he spilled this data over the wire with a thousand assurances. Tardily, the Coast Guard guessed that in a case of kidnaping, if it could be proved, they could act.

Lucky looked at Flynn. "You feel all right?"

"Sure."

"Look here, that dive bomber has full racks. We'll stop that steamer at sea. It may be piracy for us and jail forever, but—"

"What about Dixie?"

"We'll solve that when we come to it. Gas up and let's go!"

Twenty minutes later the all-metal plane zoomed out of the dust of the field, banked and, full out, streaked twenty degrees short of south, ASI flickering at six miles a minute. Lucky had figured out, as close as possible, the intersection of courses.

The afternoon was free from haze. Few clouds marred the turquoise of the sky. Below, the waves made an even crisscross pattern on the painfully bright bay.

The steamer had had to sail south, the length of the Chesapeake Bay, but Lucky took a corner off Delaware, raced over Maryland's Eastern Shore and was presently roaring over the Atlantic, leaving the friendly coast far behind.

His mathematics told him that this, a land plane, could travel one thousand miles without refueling, and that he would probably cover that without again seeing the shore. Failure was, in any case, his goal, unless he could get the bomber to float until the Coast Guard came up. That is, if the Coast Guard ever found him.

Enveloped in the monotony of wide and watery horizons, he began to realize what a small chance he had of ever finding the steamer. Somewhere within a circle at least two hundred miles in diameter, the vessel, if he sighted it at all, would look no bigger than a match floating on the water.

He went up to fifteen thousand to increase his visibility and bless the lack of clouds.

"There's a steamer!" yelled Flynn into the tube.

The bomber veered from its course, dashing toward the faint smudge, rolling back the curve of the world.

"Nix," said Flynn. "Great White Fleet."

The bomber snapped back to an easterly route.

For ten minutes they spotted nothing and then Flynn shouted, "A plane down around five thousand, to the south of us, heading east."

"Anything else?"

Flynn adjusted his binoculars, stared for a moment and then yelped, "It's the same ship that attacked us over Virginia!"

"Good! He can't see us. We're too high in the sun. Smith started later than I thought, and he's bound to know where that steamer is. We'll pull the throttle a notch."

"We haven't anything to fight with, Lucky."

"We've got the wing guns, haven't we?"

"But I ain't got anything back here. Look at him, Lucky. Cold meat!"

Easing back to two-eighty, the evident speed of the gray pursuit ship below and ahead, Lucky tagged hopefully.

"That pursuit ship was never built in America," volunteered Flynn. "Too square. Too many wires."

"We know where it was built." It was four o'clock before a smudge could be seen ahead. The spring day was almost over. Night would fall before the bomber could get more than halfway to land and the gas would be gone long before that time—and the bomber would ride waves less than two hours.

"Oh, for a radio," mourned Flynn. "Even if we win, we lose."

"Is that the right freighter?" said Lucky.

Flynn methodically inspected it with his binoculars and declared that it was. "She's flying the American flag, too, the damned pirates."

The ship was five miles ahead and three miles down, about the size of a needle floating in a glass of water, black smoke no more than a dot against the enormous bowl of the sea.

The gray pursuit ship was a gnat flitting through the dusk, almost invisible against the pattern of the waves.

The sunset was turning to flame, the sky was deepening to indigo in the direction of Africa.

The waves were long, thin shadows, as close together as the threads of black gauze.

Presently the white wake disappeared as the steamer swung to. Smith would land in the sea, to be picked up by a lifeboat.

Flynn could see the davits swing out and then he shouted, "They must have sighted us! They're signaling Smith not to land!"

"We'll bomb first and fight second," said Lucky.

"But with Smith still in the air to pick us off—"

"We'll take that chance."

Lucky opened the engine wide, and the gleaming plane, blood-red in the setting sun, leaped ahead, a Pegasus stung by a spur.

The gray ship banked in a climbing turn, scrambling for altitude.

Fifteen thousand feet under the dive bomber, three miles straight down, the steamer began to get under weigh once more, rapidly picking up speed, already starting a zigzag.

Verticaling tightly, tipping the sea until it was certain that all the water would run out of it, Lucky looked sideways at the faraway vessel.

Flynn was busy with the binoculars. "Three machine guns mounted aft, all manned and waitin' for us. It sure ain't much of a bomb target; I'd rather shoot at a mile-away penny."

"See any sign of Dixie?"

"There's something white—"

"She was wearing a light-colored polo coat, wasn't she?"

"That's her!" cried Flynn. "They got her on the forward well deck, just ahead of the superstructure. Good God, Lucky, we can't bomb that ship!"

"Forward well, is it. We'll bomb aft."

"But, Lucky, a pullout at three thousand . . . We don't know if we can hit the afterdeck!"

"We won't pull out at three thousand. Hold your breath. We're going down!"

CHAPTER ELEVEN

The Ship Shows Her Mettle

F LYNN'S agonized protest was blasted aside by the rising snarl of the engine.

The dive bomber went over the hump and then, like a silver arrow, shot itself against the sea.

Up, up, up sirened the engine. Down, down, down flashed the wings. Up to terminal velocity, back on the throttle. No engine on earth could drive the ship any faster now. Air was a solid wall against the cowling, shrieking, ripped asunder by the racing bullet's thunder.

The steamer grew longer. The sea was a bowl, a whirlpool. Lucky could see the masts, then the halyards, then the caulked seams in the planking.

The gray pursuit whipped by, left at five thousand feet as though standing still. It came around, nosed over, opened up and started after them, hopelessly lost for the moment, but ready the instant Lucky came out.

The weave of the coiled hawsers could be clearly seen. Men were staring up with frightened faces. Grim-visaged gunners began to shoot at the perfect target, the .50-caliber weapons spilling a stream of glittering brass to the decks, hosing lead and flame into the sky.

Down, down, down sped the dive bomber.

Lucky sighted on the after hatch. He did not dare glance forward at Dixie.

The zigzagging steamer rolled hastily out of the way but sure hands on rudders and stick placed the quarterdeck again between the two front cylinders without faltering.

Noise hammered the world. A bolt of lightning with thunder as well.

Flynn knew when to pull. The instant he felt the ship start out of the dive. Holding the releases, light as a feather in his seat, ready to pull and yell all at the same time, Flynn saw them go lower than three thousand.

Two thousand! One thousand!

He could count the buttons on Bullard's vest. Would Lucky stay in the groove forever?

Five hundred, four hundred, almost as low as the pennants, almost level with the scared sailor in the crow's-nest.

Lucky knew he could not afford to miss. At seven hundred feet per second, the timing would have to be perfection itself.

He eased the stick. Flynn yanked the releases.

Thrown like pebbles from a sling, five bombs threw themselves at the triangle made by the three machine guns.

Lucky yelled and hauled out. The fist which was split air banged against the wings and fuselage. Waves licked for the withdrawn wheels.

Lucky kept the stick back. Like a pole-vaulter, he shot skyward again, straight up.

Over his shoulder and down, he saw flame and smoke and steel fly up from the stern of the freighter, to hang in a cloud as suddenly lazy as it had been violent.

Over his shoulder and down, he saw flame and smoke and steel fly up from the stern of the freighter, to hang in a cloud as suddenly lazy as it had been violent.

It was impossible to see anything through that haze now. Impossible to tell if he had sunk the vessel outright.

Flynn yelled, "The plane!"

The same instant, metal sang, pierced by stabbing lead.

Lucky went over on his back in a loop, upending the sea completely, mingling sunset with smoke, waves with wings.

Upside down, looking straight ahead, he saw the gray ship.

The wing guns let drive. The pursuit dodged frantically to the left.

Lucky rolled and banked and fastened the other plane's tail through the gleaming disc of the prop.

Wing guns started up again.

"Cold meat!" shouted Flynn.

The dive bomber overrode the other plane, slapped it with the shadow of wings. Lucky looked down at Smith, but Smith did not look up.

Even in that fraction of a second, Lucky saw that Smith would no longer contemplate shooting pilots in the back. There was very little left of Smith's head.

The gray ship slopped over on one wing, straightened out and then whipstalled. With engine still on, it began its final dive, describing a corkscrew.

Lucky circled and presently the gray ship hit with a geyser of spray, almost instantly gone below the surface of the waves.

But Lucky had become aware of a certain clanking sound in his ship's engine, a certain smell.

Either Smith or a machine gunner on the steamer had got the bomber's gas tanks.

A fine spray of the fluid was whipping back from the left wing like a veil, and before Lucky could say anything to Flynn, the engine quit entirely and left them in a sibilant void.

"Here," said Lucky, "is where we find out if one of these things will float."

"Might as well add that to the tests. She hangs together in a dive, she bombs perfect and she bested a pursuit job, so we may as well know *all* about it," said Flynn.

Lucky felt out the best gliding angle and started their descent. After the steady shriek of wind and the bellow of the engine and the racketing blast of guns, the quiet was very welcome.

The molten, scarlet sun was down, leaving a twilight haze. Lucky tried not to think about Dixie. He was not sure that all the bombs had gone where Flynn had tried to place them. A dull dread filled him.

The freighter was very much afloat, though it was easily seen that she would cruise no further until a dry dock had repaired her stern. Steering engines, possibly the shafts themselves, were blown away.

Floating with a high bow and showing no signs of sinking, the vessel rolled a little to the south of the spot where Lucky was landing.

Without letting down his wheels, choosing to take a crest and try it crosswind, Lucky settled into the spray. . . .

CHAPTER TWELVE

Dixie's Fate

TOSSED alternately from tip to trough, the bomber lurched drunkenly, shipping water, nose up, then tail up, with the black combers cleaning their fangs for the final bite.

Lucky had little hope of ever knowing Dixie's fate. His own was definite.

"Sorry?" he asked Flynn.

"We got them, didn't we? They won't go noplace now."

"Look, what's that?" said Lucky.

He slid back his hood and stood up in the giddy cockpit, salt spray biting at him.

A lifeboat from the freighter was coming in toward them. A man who held a submachine gun yelled, "Take this line!"

Lucky was astounded, until he bethought himself that Bullard would hardly let a bomber go to waste in this shameful fashion.

The lifeboat, motor-driven, took the slowly sinking bomber in tow. Lucky did not think they would reach the bobbing hull of the vessel. But fate was being either kind or unkind, depending upon the reception.

They came abreast of the forward deck, and a boom with slings dangling was lowered down to them. Lucky and Flynn, getting very wet in the process, made the best of things and secured the ropes to the plane. The boom lifted away and in a moment the dripping wings were over the ship, swinging in toward the big, square hatch.

Bullard roared, "You'll get yours, Martin—and you too, Flynn. No guys are going to— Hey, Svenson, you got that jury rudder rigged yet?"

"Yust about," somebody said from the bridge.

Jury rudder? Then the ship could still proceed? They hadn't stopped them? Lucky's heart sank.

Men dragged him down from the cockpit and Bullard ranged up. But before Bullard said anything more, Dixie brushed him aside and threw her arms around Lucky.

"Get away from him," cried Bullard, thrusting her aside.

Lucky saw Bullard's face plainly for the first time. Bullard had a scratch which ran diagonally from his left eye to his thick mouth. Dixie turned to face him, and Bullard dodged.

"You got Smith, did you?" said Bullard. "And you tried to blow us out of the water, did you? Okay, Lucky Martin, you and Flynn stand over there against that bulkhead. I said stand over there!"

Lucky looked around him and saw no escape.

"Give me that Tommy gun," snapped Bullard, yanking it out of the bosun's hands. "Come on, you two. Snap it up!"

Dixie tried to speak. Flynn swallowed hard, staring at the weapon. Lucky promised himself a good crack at Bullard's jaw before he went out.

"What's that?" said the bosun.

A steady, even, drumming sound came faintly to them.

Lucky knew what it was. Bullard also knew. Savagely he sought to throw his targets into position. He had only one chance to squash the evidence.

Another sound came up on the port side.

"Ahoy! Ahoy the bridge! What the devil's going on here?"

An instant later a deadly little hundred-and-sixty-five-footer swept up to the steamer's rail. Gold braid and white caps and web-belted .45s came in a swift torrent over the side, as though the freighter had shipped a peculiarly lethal sea.

An officer, thrusting his way through the paralyzed seamen, confronted everybody in general. "Which is Martin?"

"I'm Martin."

The officer sang out, "All right, Skipper. This is the ship!"

Bullard's courage went out of him like hot air out of a balloon. He began to drool excuses and whimper and whine until even the Coast Guard was disgusted.

A big flying boat came down out of the darkness to look the situation over and then vanished into the west.

The Coast Guard lieutenant and his men rounded up all hands with speed and dispatch. They pried into the hold and found what the crates contained. They took a set of lines from the patrol ship and prepared to ride the night.

Later, in the steamer's cabin, with all quiet and under control, Dixie and Lucky faced each other across the table. Because the lieutenant was there, drinking a cup of coffee, and because, after all, it's against the rules for anyone connected with flying to show emotion of any kind, the two said their sentences with their eyes.

"Good job you did," remarked the lieutenant breezily.

"You didn't see it, did you?" said Lucky in surprise.

"Me? Oh, not me—I was in the radio room listening to Jenson. He's the pilot of that flying boat that went over. When you started your dive, he picked you out by the sun on your wings. It was pretty low, you know. And he built altitude pretty fast and saw what you did, and he told us about it. We sent him out first thing, but he isn't as fast as your plane. He spotted us to this place, staying a long way off while he did it, because he could hardly attack with a .45, you know."

"Do you think," said Dixie, "that Jenson might tell the Navy about it?"

"Oh, sure."

"Then," said Dixie, "then Lawson will know it *did* stay together."

"You bet he will," said Lucky.

"That was a swell scrap you had with that other ship," said the lieutenant.

"There's the evidence," said Dixie.

"And we've got a hundred planes in the hold," said Lucky, "all ready to peddle to the place where they belong. Dixie—"

"What?"

There was something of a silence, and then the lieutenant casually set his cup on the table and wandered away, just as though he had thought of something important which had to be done.

Story Preview

Story Preview

NOW that you've just ventured through one of the captivating tales in the Stories from the Golden Age collection by L. Ron Hubbard, turn the page and enjoy a preview of *The Lieutenant Takes the Sky*. Join American pilot Mike Malloy, who enlisted in the French Foreign Legion only to get himself thrown into a Moroccan military jail for trying to swab a deck with a general's aide. To get out of prison and clear his name, Malloy undertakes a suicide mission: to fly deep into enemy territory and find an alchemist's book missing for 800 years, a discovery that may determine the destiny of a nation.

The Lieutenant Takes the Sky

CAPTAIN Mike Malloy was conducted to the general's office with great speed. Before the door, the files grounded their Lebels with a loud crash and the corporal threw the portal wide.

The people in the office turned. General LeRoi gave a start and scowled.

He had not expected his order to be so promptly carried out, and he had never imagined for an instant that Captain Mike Malloy of the French Air Service could be anything but neat. Just now, Mike was not at all polished. A week in jail had taken away all gloss. His beard was dark; his tunic was ripped from shoulder to waist, and the flapping cloth almost obscured his pilot's wings; the bill of his dusty kepi was broken and, all in all, his condition yelled, "Dungeons!"

But for all that Mike was cool enough. He pushed his kepi to the back of his head and walked out of the guard file and into the office. He stopped before the general's desk, looking neither right nor left.

"You sent for me, sir?"

"I did!" said LeRoi, white mustaches bristling and ruddy face scarlet. "You seem to be somewhat untidy."

"No illusion about it," said Mike. "Your observation is correct."

LeRoi coughed and glared, and then gradually composed himself through necessity.

"Captain Malloy, I wish to introduce you to *M'm'selle* Lois DuGanne," said the general.

Mike turned and then blushed for the wretchedness of his appearance. Lois DuGanne, a little bewildered, nodded to him and gave him a slight smile. Mike bowed but he did not lower his glance. She was a very lovely woman, all neat and crisp in delicate whites. Her eyes were blue and frank. Mike was spellbound.

The general coughed to distract Mike's attention.

"And," said LeRoi loudly, "I wish to present you to *M.* Delage, and his secretary, Henri Corvault."

Mike turned to shake Delage's hand. The man was patently important. His linen was expensive, and was cut on the pattern of most French politicians'. He was around forty, and there was a certain arresting quality about him which one could trace to his eyes. They were odd, those eyes, because it was impossible to tell their exact color.

Henri, the secretary, was too thin to throw a decent shadow. His head was too big for his body and his neck too small. He seemed to be a very timid echo of Delage.

"Captain Malloy," said General LeRoi, "is the man I have been telling you about. He has just returned from scout duty and I apologize for his appearance. However, it has nothing to do with his competence. He knows every square inch of the Middle Atlas, having fought throughout the last campaign in that region, and he is one of our best pilots."

Mike looked on in amazement and heard in astonishment such praise.

"In addition, we will send with you our Lieutenant Reynard, who is also an excellent pilot," continued LeRoi. "I doubt you will suffer any inconveniences on your trip."

Delage stood up. "General, I am very pleased at your generosity. I could have hoped for nothing more satisfactory."

"*M*. Delage," said the general, "it is with extreme pleasure that I am able to extend to you the courtesies of the French Army. It is little enough to do for such an important personage as yourself."

They bowed to each other.

Miss DuGanne stood up. "And I too thank you, General."

"*M'm'selle,*" said LeRoi, "while I regret your insistence upon accompanying the party into the Middle Atlas—which I assure you is no place for a lovely woman—I shall nevertheless do all in my power to aid you."

Henri scuttled to the door and opened it for Delage. The personage bowed in the entrance to the general and then to Mike. "We shall see you in the morning, Captain."

Miss DuGanne smiled at the two officers and withdrew.

When the door had closed, Mike looked with suspicion at LeRoi. "If you don't mind my saying so, sir, it's hardly the time for an expedition of a private sort—"

"Nobody asked your opinion," snapped LeRoi, sitting down. "Why did they have to bring you here in that condition! If you could see yourself . . . !"

"Sir, I assure you that if I had had time, and if I had known,

I would have presented another facet of my glittering self. But your guards are most abrupt and your jail . . . General, you should look into that jail."

"None of your insolence, Malloy. You were brought here for one purpose and one purpose only. You can go to the *bataillon pénal,* as scheduled, or you can fly this party into the Middle Atlas. I give you that choice."

Mike was suspicious. "By any chance, would the Middle Atlas trip be worse than the *bataillon pénal*?"

"Probably," snapped LeRoi. "You know the conditions inland as well as I do. Berbers sniping at planes, strange troop movements, and the lid about to blow off all Morocco. I chose you because I would not order an officer on such duty—"

"You are ordering Lieutenant Reynard," said Mike.

"Yes, Lieutenant Reynard. He has committed one too many murders in the name of espionage. As he cannot be censured for doing his duty, I can only send him on such a mission."

Mike was very puzzled by now. "Sir, if it is going to be as bad as all that, how can you send such an important man as *M.* Delage into the interior—"

"I send him nowhere," corrected LeRoi. "*M.* Delage is much less important than he himself thinks. He is a small-time politician in France, has some remote connection with the French Academy and, through ignorance, has selected this time to go searching for a book in the Middle Atlas."

"A book?" said Mike.

"Yes. I understand that it is the girl's idea. She is an American and, like you, seems to be crazy. The book is *L'Aud,* the only volume missing from the Karaouine University Library. It has been gone for eight hundred years, and was last in the possession of Sultan Ibn Tumart. I believe it contained an alchemical formula for the manufacture of gold from base metals. That is all pure bosh, but these three people are crazy to go on their trip, and they have asked the French Army to help them. Very well, help them we shall. But they will also help us."

To find out more about *The Lieutenant Takes the Sky* and how you can obtain your copy, go to www.goldenagestories.com.

Glossary

STORIES FROM THE GOLDEN AGE *reflect the words and expressions used in the 1930s and 1940s, adding unique flavor and authenticity to the tales. While a character's speech may often reflect regional origins, it also can convey attitudes common in the day. So that readers can better grasp such cultural and historical terms, uncommon words or expressions of the era, the following glossary has been provided.*

---

altimeter: a gauge that measures altitude.

alum: a colorless crystalline compound used as an astringent, which shrinks body tissue it is applied to. Used figuratively.

Anacostia River: a river in the District of Columbia about twenty-four miles (thirty-nine km) long. The name derives from the Anacostan Indians who settled on the banks of the river.

ASI: airspeed indicator.

astern, two-thirds speed: to go backward at two-thirds the standard ship speed, which is approximately ten knots or eleven and a half miles (eighteen and a half km) per hour. Used figuratively.

bataillon pénal: (French) penal battalion; military unit consisting of convicted persons for whom military service was either assigned punishment or a voluntary replacement of imprisonment. Penal battalion service was very dangerous: the official view was that they were highly expendable and were to be used to reduce losses in regular units. Convicts were released from their term of service early if they suffered a combat injury (the crime was considered to be "washed out with blood") or performed a heroic deed.

Battery, the: a landmark promenade that stretches along the shores of the Charleston, South Carolina peninsula. It was used as a place for artillery during the Civil War.

Berbers: members of a people living in North Africa, primarily Muslim, living in settled or nomadic tribes between the Sahara and Mediterranean Sea and between Egypt and the Atlantic Ocean.

Bolling: Bolling Field; located in southwest Washington, DC and officially opened in 1918, it was named in honor of the first high-ranking air service officer killed in World War I. Bolling served as a research and testing ground for new aviation equipment and its first mission provided aerial defense of the capital.

bosun: a ship's officer in charge of supervision and maintenance of the ship and its equipment.

canister: a metallic cylinder packed with shot that scatters upon discharge from a cannon, formerly used as an anti-personnel round. Used figuratively.

chronometer: an instrument for measuring time accurately in spite of motion or varying conditions.

cotillion: a brisk, lively dance characterized by many intricate steps and the continual changing of partners. Used figuratively.

cowl or **cowling:** the removable metal housing of an aircraft engine, often designed as part of the airplane's body, containing the cockpit, passenger seating and cargo but excluding the wings.

crate: an airplane.

crow's-nest: a platform or shelter for a lookout at or near the top of a mast.

Cyclone: type of engine used extensively in large air transports and military aircraft.

davits: any of various cranelike devices, used singly or in pairs, for supporting, raising and lowering boats, anchors and cargo over a hatchway or side of a ship.

Department of Commerce: the department of the US federal government that promotes and administers domestic and foreign commerce. In 1926, Congress passed an Air Commerce Act that gave the US Department of Commerce some regulation over air facilities, the authority to establish air traffic rules and the authority to issue licenses and certificates.

dry behind the ears, hardly: "not dry behind the ears," a contemptuous expression, applied to a young person; inexperienced.

Duralumin: a strong low-density aluminum alloy used especially in aircraft.

Eastern Air or **EAT:** Eastern Air Transport; former US airline that served primarily the eastern US. It was a composite of several air travel corporations established in 1926. In 1930 it was named Eastern Air Transport and later became Eastern Air Lines.

elevator fin: a hinged horizontal surface on an airplane at the tail end of the fuselage that is used to produce motion up or down.

fire, Gridley: refers to Charles Vernon Gridley (1844–1898); US naval officer who started the Battle of Manila Bay in the Spanish-American War with the order from his commanding officer, "You may fire when you are ready, Gridley." The Spanish fleet was annihilated without the loss of a single American life. This dramatic victory eventually led to the US annexation of the Philippines.

flivver: a small, cheap and usually old car.

flying boat: a seaplane whose main body is a hull adapted for floating.

Fort Sumter: a fort at the entrance to the harbor of Charleston, South Carolina and the location of the first military engagement of the Civil War.

G: gravity; a unit of acceleration equal to the acceleration of gravity at the Earth's surface.

G-men: government men; agents of the Federal Bureau of Investigation.

grandstanding: playing or acting so as to impress onlookers.

Great White Fleet: US Navy; popular nickname for the white-hulled US Navy battle fleet that completed a circumnavigation of the world between 1907 and 1909

106

by order of President Theodore Roosevelt. It consisted of four squadrons of four battleships each. Roosevelt sought to demonstrate the growing American military power and force capable of operating across the deep waters of open oceans.

half-winger: refers to the rear-seat crew member in a two-seat bomber, fighter or observation aircraft. A half-winger is not a qualified pilot. Their insignia consisted of the letter "O" with a single wing attached to one side of the letter.

halyards: ropes used for raising and lowering sails.

Hampton Roads: deep-water channel and commercial waterway in southeastern Virginia on the Chesapeake Bay. It is one of the country's busiest ports and shipbuilding centers.

hawsers: cables or ropes used in mooring or towing ships.

Ibn Tumart: (1080–1130) Berber religious teacher and founder of the ruling dynasty of the twelfth century in the region that is now Morocco. He founded a monastery in the Atlas Mountains that served as an important religious center. It is also his burial site.

jury rudder: a rudder constructed for temporary use.

Karaouine University Library: university in Fez, Morocco, founded in 859 and one of the oldest universities in the world. It is associated with the city's giant mosque and is considered one of the most important centers of learning in North Africa.

kopek: a monetary unit of Russia equal to one-hundredth of a ruble.

Lebels: French rifles that were adopted as standard infantry weapons in 1887 and remained in official service until after World War II.

M. or *M'sieu:* (French) *Monsieur*; French title equivalent to Mister.

Mex: Mexican peso; in 1732 it was introduced as a trade coin with China and was so popular that China became one of its principal consumers. Mexico minted and exported pesos to China until 1949. It was issued as both coins and paper money.

Middle Atlas: part of the Atlas Mountain range lying in Morocco. It is the westernmost of three Atlas Mountain chains that define a large plateaued basin extending eastward into Algeria.

M'm'selle: (French) *Mademoiselle*; an unmarried woman or girl; the French title equivalent to Miss.

mooring mast: the mast or tower to which a dirigible is moored. Used figuratively.

Mount Vernon: an estate of northeast Virginia on the Potomac River near Washington, DC. It was the home of George Washington from 1752 until his death in 1799.

Neutrality Laws: laws governing a country's abstention from participating in a conflict or aiding a participant of such conflict, and the duty of participants to refrain from violating the territory, seizing the possession of, or hampering the peaceful commerce of the neutral countries.

Norfolk: port city located in southeastern Virginia on the Elizabeth River at the mouth of the Chesapeake Bay.

off his feed: suffering a lack of appetite; sick.

quarterdeck: the rear part of the upper deck of a ship, usually reserved for officers.

queer: to ruin or thwart.

ring mount: a rotating mount on an aircraft that allowed the gun to be turned to any direction with the gunner remaining directly behind it.

roadster: an open-top automobile with a single seat in front for two or three persons, a fabric top and either a luggage compartment or a rumble seat in back. A rumble seat is an upholstered exterior seat with a hinged lid that opens to form the back of the seat when in use.

Rock of Gibraltar: projection of land 1,396 feet (425.5 meters) high, off the southwestern tip of Europe on the Iberian peninsula. Despite long sieges it seemed that there was nothing that could destroy the rock or its people. This history has inspired the saying "solid as the Rock of Gibraltar" that is used to describe a person or situation that cannot be overcome and does not fail.

Rough Rider: used figuratively to mean a member of the first US volunteer cavalry recruited in 1898 by Theodore Roosevelt, composed of seasoned ranch hands and expert athletes. They became famous for their bold and daring attack on the Spanish in the Battle of San Juan Hill (Cuba) during the Spanish-American War. Members became national heroes and many were awarded the Medal of Honor, the highest military decoration bestowed upon a member of the armed forces for gallantry and risk of his life above and beyond the call of duty.

rudder: a device used to steer ships or aircraft. A rudder is a flat plane or sheet of material attached with hinges to the craft's stern or tail. In typical aircraft, pedals operate rudders via mechanical linkages.

rumble: rumble seat; an upholstered exterior seat in the back of a car with a hinged lid that opens to form the back of the seat when in use.

Scheherazade: the female narrator of *The Arabian Nights,* who during one thousand and one adventurous nights saved her life by entertaining her husband, the king, with stories.

Sing Sing: a maximum security prison approximately thirty miles north of New York City in the town of Ossining. The name comes from the original name of the town that was "Sing Sing."

slipstream: the airstream pushed back by a revolving aircraft propeller.

stall: a situation in which an aircraft suddenly dives because the airflow is obstructed and lift is lost. The loss of airflow can be caused by insufficient airspeed or by an excessive angle of an airfoil (part of an aircraft's surface that provides lift or control) when the aircraft is climbing.

struts: supports for a structure such as an aircraft wing, roof or bridge.

superstructure: cabins and rooms above the deck of a ship.

tab trim: the adjustment of the tab, a small, adjustable hinged surface, located on the trailing edge of the aileron, rudder or elevator control surface. It is adjusted by the pilot to maintain balance and to help stabilize the aircraft in flight.

tarmac: airport runway.

tars: sailors.

terminal velocity: the constant speed that a falling object reaches when the downward gravitational force equals the frictional resistance of the medium through which it is falling, usually air.

thirty-thirty: .30-30; a cartridge approximately .30" in diameter, originally having a powder charge of 30 grains, which is the source of its name.

three-mile limit: the outer limit of the area extending three miles out to sea from the coast of a country, sometimes considered to constitute the country's territorial waters.

Tommy gun: Thompson submachine gun; a light portable automatic machine gun.

tracer: a bullet or shell whose course is made visible by a trail of flames or smoke, used to assist in aiming.

Treasury Department: an executive department of the US federal government, which in addition to administering the treasury of the US government also carries out certain law enforcement activities, including investigating and prosecuting smugglers, gun law violators and other threats to national security.

under the hammer: for sale at public auction.

under weigh: in motion; underway.

well deck: the space on the main deck of a ship lying at a lower level between the bridge and either a raised forward deck or a raised deck at the stern, which usually has cabins underneath.

Western Front: term used during World War I and II to describe the "contested armed frontier" (otherwise known as "the front") between lands controlled by the Germans to the East and the Allies to the West. In World War I, both sides dug in along a meandering line of fortified trenches stretching from the coast of the North Sea, southward to the Swiss border that was the Western Front. This line remained essentially unchanged for most of the war. In 1918 the relentless advance of the Allied armies persuaded the German commanders that defeat was inevitable and the government was forced to request armistice.

whipstall: a maneuver in a small aircraft in which it goes into a vertical climb, pauses briefly, and then drops toward the earth, nose first.

windsock: a fabric tube or cone attached at one end to the top of a pole to show which way the wind is blowing.

wingover: also known as the Immelmann turn; an aerial maneuver named after World War I flying ace Max Immelmann. The pilot pulls the aircraft into a vertical climb, applying full rudder as the speed drops, then rolls the aircraft while pulling back slightly on the stick, causing the aircraft to dive back down in the opposite direction. It has become one of the most popular aerial maneuvers in the world.

Yank: Yankee; term used to refer to Americans in general.

L. Ron Hubbard
in the Golden Age
of Pulp Fiction

In writing an adventure story
a writer has to know that he is adventuring
for a lot of people who cannot.
The writer has to take them here and there
about the globe and show them
excitement and love and realism.
As long as that writer is living the part of an
adventurer when he is hammering
the keys, he is succeeding with his story.

Adventuring is a state of mind.
If you adventure through life, you have a
good chance to be a success on paper.

Adventure doesn't mean globe-trotting,
exactly, and it doesn't mean great deeds.
Adventuring is like art.
You have to live it to make it real.

—L. RON HUBBARD

L. Ron Hubbard
and American
Pulp Fiction

B ORN March 13, 1911, L. Ron Hubbard lived a life at
least as expansive as the stories with which he enthralled
a hundred million readers through a fifty-year career.

Originally hailing from Tilden, Nebraska, he spent his
formative years in a classically rugged Montana, replete with
the cowpunchers, lawmen and desperadoes who would later
people his Wild West adventures. And lest anyone imagine
those adventures were drawn from vicarious experience, he
was not only breaking broncs at a tender age, he was also
among the few whites ever admitted into Blackfoot society
as a bona fide blood brother. While if only to round out an
otherwise rough and tumble youth, his mother was that rarity
of her time—a thoroughly educated woman—who introduced
her son to the classics of Occidental literature even before his
seventh birthday.

But as any dedicated L. Ron Hubbard reader will attest, his
world extended far beyond Montana. In point of fact, and as the
son of a United States naval officer, by the age of eighteen he
had traveled over a quarter of a million miles. Included therein
were three Pacific crossings to a then still mysterious Asia, where
he ran with the likes of Her British Majesty's agent-in-place

L. Ron Hubbard, left, at Congressional Airport, Washington, DC, 1931, with members of George Washington University flying club.

for North China, and the last in the line of Royal Magicians from the court of Kublai Khan. For the record, L. Ron Hubbard was also among the first Westerners to gain admittance to forbidden Tibetan monasteries below Manchuria, and his photographs of China's Great Wall long graced American geography texts.

Upon his return to the United States and a hasty completion of his interrupted high school education, the young Ron Hubbard entered George Washington University. There, as fans of his aerial adventures may have heard, he earned his wings as a pioneering barnstormer at the dawn of American aviation. He also earned a place in free-flight record books for the longest sustained flight above Chicago. Moreover, as a roving reporter for *Sportsman Pilot* (featuring his first professionally penned articles), he further helped inspire a generation of pilots who would take America to world airpower.

Immediately beyond his sophomore year, Ron embarked on the first of his famed ethnological expeditions, initially to then untrammeled Caribbean shores (descriptions of which would later fill a whole series of West Indies mystery-thrillers). That the Puerto Rican interior would also figure into the future of Ron Hubbard stories was likewise no accident. For in addition to cultural studies of the island, a 1932–33

LRH expedition is rightly remembered as conducting the first complete mineralogical survey of a Puerto Rico under United States jurisdiction.

There was many another adventure along this vein: As a lifetime member of the famed Explorers Club, L. Ron Hubbard charted North Pacific waters with the first shipboard radio direction finder, and so pioneered a long-range navigation system universally employed until the late twentieth century. While not to put too fine an edge on it, he also held a rare Master Mariner's license to pilot any vessel, of any tonnage in any ocean.

Yet lest we stray too far afield, there is an LRH note at this juncture in his saga, and it reads in part:

"I started out writing for the pulps, writing the best I knew, writing for every mag on the stands, slanting as well as I could."

To which one might add: His earliest submissions date from the summer of 1934, and included tales drawn from true-to-life Asian adventures, with characters roughly modeled on British/American intelligence operatives he had known in Shanghai. His early Westerns were similarly peppered with details drawn from personal experience. Although therein lay a first hard lesson from the often cruel world of the pulps. His first Westerns were soundly rejected as lacking the authenticity of a Max Brand yarn

Capt. L. Ron Hubbard in Ketchikan, Alaska, 1940, on his Alaskan Radio Experimental Expedition, the first of three voyages conducted under the Explorers Club flag.

(a particularly frustrating comment given L. Ron Hubbard's Westerns came straight from his Montana homeland, while Max Brand was a mediocre New York poet named Frederick Schiller Faust, who turned out implausible six-shooter tales from the terrace of an Italian villa).

Nevertheless, and needless to say, L. Ron Hubbard persevered and soon earned a reputation as among the most publishable names in pulp fiction, with a ninety percent placement rate of first-draft manuscripts. He was also among the most prolific, averaging between seventy and a hundred thousand words a month. Hence the rumors that L. Ron Hubbard had redesigned a typewriter for faster keyboard action and pounded out manuscripts on a continuous roll of butcher paper to save the precious seconds it took to insert a single sheet of paper into manual typewriters of the day.

That all L. Ron Hubbard stories did not run beneath said byline is yet another aspect of pulp fiction lore. That is, as publishers periodically rejected manuscripts from top-drawer authors if only to avoid paying top dollar, L. Ron Hubbard and company just as frequently replied with submissions under various pseudonyms. In Ron's case, the list

A MAN OF MANY NAMES

Between 1934 and 1950, L. Ron Hubbard authored more than fifteen million words of fiction in more than two hundred classic publications. To supply his fans and editors with stories across an array of genres and pulp titles, he adopted fifteen pseudonyms in addition to his already renowned L. Ron Hubbard byline.

Winchester Remington Colt
Lt. Jonathan Daly
Capt. Charles Gordon
Capt. L. Ron Hubbard
Bernard Hubbel
Michael Keith
Rene Lafayette
Legionnaire 148
Legionnaire 14830
Ken Martin
Scott Morgan
Lt. Scott Morgan
Kurt von Rachen
Barry Randolph
Capt. Humbert Reynolds

included: Rene Lafayette, Captain Charles Gordon, Lt. Scott Morgan and the notorious Kurt von Rachen—supposedly on the lam for a murder rap, while hammering out two-fisted prose in Argentina. The point: While L. Ron Hubbard as Ken Martin spun stories of Southeast Asian intrigue, LRH as Barry Randolph authored tales of romance on the Western range—which, stretching between a dozen genres is how he came to stand among the two hundred elite authors providing close to a million tales through the glory days of American Pulp Fiction.

L. Ron Hubbard, circa 1930, at the outset of a literary career that would finally span half a century.

In evidence of exactly that, by 1936 L. Ron Hubbard was literally leading pulp fiction's elite as president of New York's American Fiction Guild. Members included a veritable pulp hall of fame: Lester "Doc Savage" Dent, Walter "The Shadow" Gibson, and the legendary Dashiell Hammett—to cite but a few.

Also in evidence of just where L. Ron Hubbard stood within his first two years on the American pulp circuit: By the spring of 1937, he was ensconced in Hollywood, adopting a Caribbean thriller for Columbia Pictures, remembered today as *The Secret of Treasure Island.* Comprising fifteen thirty-minute episodes, the L. Ron Hubbard screenplay led to the most profitable matinée serial in Hollywood history. In accord with Hollywood culture, he was thereafter continually called

119

The 1937 Secret of Treasure Island, *a fifteen-episode serial adapted for the screen by L. Ron Hubbard from his novel,* Murder at Pirate Castle.

upon to rewrite/doctor scripts—most famously for long-time friend and fellow adventurer Clark Gable.

In the interim—and herein lies another distinctive chapter of the L. Ron Hubbard story—he continually worked to open Pulp Kingdom gates to up-and-coming authors. Or, for that matter, anyone who wished to write. It was a fairly unconventional stance, as markets were already thin and competition razor sharp. But the fact remains, it was an L. Ron Hubbard hallmark that he vehemently lobbied on behalf of young authors—regularly supplying instructional articles to trade journals, guest-lecturing to short story classes at George Washington University and Harvard, and even founding his own creative writing competition. It was established in 1940, dubbed the Golden Pen, and guaranteed winners both New York representation and publication in *Argosy*.

But it was John W. Campbell Jr.'s *Astounding Science Fiction* that finally proved the most memorable LRH vehicle. While every fan of L. Ron Hubbard's galactic epics undoubtedly knows the story, it nonetheless bears repeating: By late 1938, the pulp publishing magnate of Street & Smith was determined to revamp *Astounding Science Fiction* for broader readership. In particular, senior editorial director F. Orlin Tremaine called for stories with a stronger *human element*. When acting editor John W. Campbell balked, preferring his spaceship-driven tales,

Tremaine enlisted Hubbard. Hubbard, in turn, replied with the genre's first truly *character-driven* works, wherein heroes are pitted not against bug-eyed monsters but the mystery and majesty of deep space itself—and thus was launched the Golden Age of Science Fiction.

The names alone are enough to quicken the pulse of any science fiction aficionado, including LRH friend and protégé, Robert Heinlein, Isaac Asimov, A. E. van Vogt and Ray Bradbury. Moreover, when coupled with LRH stories of fantasy, we further come to what's rightly been described as the foundation of every modern tale of horror: L. Ron Hubbard's immortal *Fear*. It was rightly proclaimed by Stephen King as one of the very few works to genuinely warrant that overworked term "classic"—as in: *"This is a classic tale of creeping, surreal menace and horror. . . . This is one of the really, really good ones."*

To accommodate the greater body of L. Ron Hubbard fantasies, Street & Smith inaugurated *Unknown*—a classic pulp if there ever was one, and wherein readers were soon thrilling to the likes of *Typewriter in the Sky* and *Slaves of Sleep* of which Frederik Pohl would declare: *"There are bits and pieces from Ron's work that became part of the language in ways that very few other writers managed."*

L. Ron Hubbard, 1948, among fellow science fiction luminaries at the World Science Fiction Convention in Toronto.

And, indeed, at J. W. Campbell Jr.'s insistence, Ron was regularly drawing on themes from the Arabian Nights and

121

so introducing readers to a world of genies, jinn, Aladdin and Sinbad—all of which, of course, continue to float through cultural mythology to this day.

At least as influential in terms of post-apocalypse stories was L. Ron Hubbard's 1940 *Final Blackout*. Generally acclaimed as the finest anti-war novel of the decade and among the ten best works of the genre ever authored—here, too, was a tale that would live on in ways few other writers

Portland, Oregon, 1943; L. Ron Hubbard captain of the US Navy subchaser PC 815.

imagined. Hence, the later Robert Heinlein verdict: "Final Blackout *is as perfect a piece of science fiction as has ever been written.*"

Like many another who both lived and wrote American pulp adventure, the war proved a tragic end to Ron's sojourn in the pulps. He served with distinction in four theaters and was highly decorated for commanding corvettes in the North Pacific. He was also grievously wounded in combat, lost many a close friend and colleague and thus resolved to say farewell to pulp fiction and devote himself to what it had supported these many years—namely, his serious research.

But in no way was the LRH literary saga at an end, for as he wrote some thirty years later, in 1980:

"Recently there came a period when I had little to do. This was novel in a life so crammed with busy years, and I decided to amuse myself by writing a novel that was pure science fiction."

That work was *Battlefield Earth: A Saga of the Year 3000.* It was an immediate *New York Times* bestseller and, in fact, the first international science fiction blockbuster in decades. It was not, however, L. Ron Hubbard's magnum opus, as that distinction is generally reserved for his next and final work: The 1.2 million word *Mission Earth.*

> **Final Blackout**
> *is as perfect
> a piece of
> science fiction as
> has ever
> been written.*
>
> —Robert Heinlein

How he managed those 1.2 million words in just over twelve months is yet another piece of the L. Ron Hubbard legend. But the fact remains, he did indeed author a ten-volume *dekalogy* that lives in publishing history for the fact that each and every volume of the series was also a *New York Times* bestseller.

Moreover, as subsequent generations discovered L. Ron Hubbard through republished works and novelizations of his screenplays, the mere fact of his name on a cover signaled an international bestseller. . . . Until, to date, sales of his works exceed hundreds of millions, and he otherwise remains among the most enduring and widely read authors in literary history. Although as a final word on the tales of L. Ron Hubbard, perhaps it's enough to simply reiterate what editors told readers in the glory days of American Pulp Fiction:

He writes the way he does, brothers, because he's been there, seen it and done it!

THE STORIES FROM THE GOLDEN AGE

Your ticket to adventure starts here with the Stories from
the Golden Age collection by master storyteller L. Ron Hubbard.
These gripping tales are set in a kaleidoscope of exotic locales and brim
with fascinating characters, including some of the
most vile villains, dangerous dames and brazen heroes
you'll ever get to meet.

The entire collection of over one hundred and fifty stories is being
released in a series of eighty books and audiobooks.
For an up-to-date listing of available titles,
go to www.goldenagestories.com.

AIR ADVENTURE

Arctic Wings	*Man-Killers of the Air*
The Battling Pilot	*On Blazing Wings*
Boomerang Bomber	*Red Death Over China*
The Crate Killer	*Sabotage in the Sky*
The Dive Bomber	*Sky Birds Dare!*
Forbidden Gold	*The Sky-Crasher*
Hurtling Wings	*Trouble on His Wings*
The Lieutenant Takes the Sky	*Wings Over Ethiopia*

FAR-FLUNG ADVENTURE

SEA ADVENTURE

TALES FROM THE ORIENT

MYSTERY

FANTASY

SCIENCE FICTION

WESTERN